THE IMPOSTOR

Maria Skinner recovers consciousness after a car crash to find herself in a psychiatric clinic. She remembers the crash quite clearly but is told that she is suffering from delusions—and must not leave the hospital.

She tries to contact her husband but is informed that he is unavailable. Finally, in a desperate attempt to escape, she reluctantly agrees to accompany a man who insists he is her husband—but who she knows is an impostor. She moves from one captivity to another—and becomes a pawn in someone else's sinister game . . .

THE IMPOSTOR

Helen McCloy

First published 1977
by
Victor Gollancz Ltd

This edition 2007 by BBC Audiobooks Ltd
published by arrangement with
the author's estate

ISBN 978 1 405 68575 7

British Library Cataloguing in Publication Data available

Printed and bound in Great Britain by
Antony Rowe Ltd., Chippenham, Wiltshire

To Bernard Manning,
Assistant Attorney General,
Commonwealth of Massachusetts,
with gratitude for his guidance
through the mazes of the law

Chapter One

Was it something in Dr. Sanders or something in Marina herself that made him hate her?

She knew that some people mistook her shyness for arrogance, but surely a psychiatrist would know the difference.

Was this just the currently fashionable love-hate paradox?

No, she would have to be obsessively vain to accept that. Common sense told her that Dr. Sanders' behavior had no more to do with love of her than Nazi behavior had to do with love of Jews.

A dark thought came to her, unbidden.

Was Eric Sanders one of those men who hate women just because they are women?

There were such men. Schopenhauer was one of them. Passing a woman, a total stranger, on a stair he was seized with such a sudden access of rage against "the short-legged race," as he called women, that he threw her down the stair, crippling her for life. The courts made him pay her a disability pension for life, which merely increased his hatred of women.

The next time Marina heard Dr. Sanders' step outside her

door she slid her hands under the bedclothes. She was not going to give him the satisfaction of seeing them tremble.

He paused in the doorway, an actor's pause calculated to heighten the impact of his entrance.

His face was long, concave, unsmiling, like the archaic faces carved out of the rock of Easter Island. In profile, brow and jaw protruded. Between them, eyes, mouth and all but the tip of the nose were depressed and shallow. The lips pouted. Such bizarre exaggeration may be tolerable in art, but it is disturbing in nature.

"Good morning, Marina." His voice was deep and resonant; his articulation, crisp.

"Good morning, Dr. Sanders."

"Won't you call me Eric?"

"I always think of you as Dr. Sanders."

"Do you shy away from familiarity with everyone?"

"No, just from familiarity with those who are not friends."

"But I am your friend, Marina." When she did not answer he went on. "How does your head feel this morning?"

"Better." Her hand rose to adjust the dressing on her forehead. "When are you going to let me go home?"

"Not until you are entirely rational."

He sat down. He was a big man, cramped in the skimpy hospital chair.

"Why doesn't my husband come to see me?"

"You are not well enough for visitors."

"Why doesn't he telephone me?"

"I have told him that any outside influence might retard your recovery."

"And he accepts that?"

"He understands that I must have complete control of my patients' environment. There is a telephone outlet in this

8

room, but no extension is plugged in."

"So I've noticed. How long have I been here?"

"Several days."

"But how many?"

"There is no need to be so precise." Dr. Sanders opened his notebook and uncapped his old-fashioned fountain pen, a handsome trifle, gold with a monogram. "Do you wish to make any changes in what you told me yesterday?"

"You asked me so many questions yesterday I can't possibly remember all I said."

"Let me refresh your memory." He put on reading glasses to glance at his notes. "You have no family except your husband. Your parents, Leah and Ralph Jacoby, are dead. Your only other relatives are cousins in California and Czechoslovakia whom you have never met. After your father's death you and your mother left Ohio for New York because you had landed a job on a magazine there called *Home Exquisite*. There was the usual conflict between your mother and yourself—"

"There was no conflict."

"Oh, come now, really, Marina!" He didn't bother to look up from his notes. "You loved your job at *Home Exquisite* and your mother hated it. Didn't she say the rooms pictured in that magazine looked as if no men, children or dogs had ever lived in them?"

"That was an office joke I had told her. She was quoting me."

"Was she?" It was one of his most irritating tricks, to repeat a statement you had just made in the form of a question loaded with disbelief. "Wasn't your mother dismayed when she found that all the people who worked with you in the editorial department were other women? Didn't she ask

9

you how you ever expected to get married if you never met any men?"

"That was a joke, too."

"Wasn't it the true word spoken in jest?"

"No, it wasn't."

He didn't reply. He just looked at her as if he believed that silent skepticism would force her to admit self-deception.

Two could play at that game. She looked at him just as silently, just as skeptically. The silence stretched until he had to break it.

"How did you first meet your husband?"

"Didn't I tell you all that yesterday?"

"I want to see if you will tell it the same way today."

"Where shall I begin?"

"With Skinner Industries."

"It's a multinational conglomerate. Among other properties, they own a string of magazines. One is called *House and Terrace*. They decided that *Home Exquisite* was unfair competition for *House and Terrace* so they bought *Home Exquisite* in order to kill it. They could have given us employees time to look for new jobs, but they didn't. So many people were thrown out of work at two weeks' notice, including me.

"The day we got the news, we held a protest meeting in the office. I was one of those who made speeches. I said pretty nasty things about Skinner Industries. There were some strangers in the back of the room listening to us. One of them applauded me and I saw him again in the elevator."

Memory was unrolling in her mind as real as a film with a sound track.

She was running to catch the elevator, breathless. He stood aside to let her enter.

10

"That was quite a speech," he said.

"You liked it?"

"No. You see my name is Victor Skinner."

"Then why did you applaud?"

"Because I liked you."

She had looked at him more closely then.

He was a tall young man who carried his height without awkwardness. There was a smile in his dark eyes. She did not return the smile.

"I do not like you," she told him. "How can you like yourself when you are part of Skinner Industries?"

"A very small part."

They had reached the lobby, but he went on talking.

"I'm just a hired hand. My grandfather started a small company called Eastern Steel eighty years ago. His grandson, my cousin Cornelius Skinner, bought out the rest of the family and collected other companies the way some men collect stamps. End product: Skinner Industries operating in thirteen countries with the head office in New York at the Skinner Building.

"I don't own stock or control policy. I have nothing to do with the Skinner magazines. I just dropped in today to see what was going on. I work for another Skinner company: Luka, Incorporated. Doesn't that make me a member of the human race?"

"I'm not sure."

"Why not have dinner with me tonight and find out?"

She had known at once that this was a turning point.

If she said no, so many things could never happen.

If she said yes, anything might happen.

She said yes. . . .

"So you were married a few months later?" said Dr. Sanders.

"Yes."

"One of those impetuous, modern courtships—a few dinners in Manhattan and a weekend in Connecticut when the forsythia was in bloom?"

"There was a little more to it than that."

"Tell me about the wedding."

"It was small. Victor's cousin, Cornelius, and his wife, Anna, couldn't come."

"Couldn't or wouldn't?"

"I don't know. They did send silver spoons. Skinner heirlooms. My mother gave me the only thing of value she had, her own engagement ring. There was only one bridesmaid, Lettice King."

"The photographers' model?"

"Yes, she had been doing some jobs for *Home Exquisite* just before it folded. She brought us a jeroboam of champagne. Victor's best man was supposed to be Cousin Cornelius' son, Thereon. At the last moment he couldn't come, but he sent us some fine old brandy in a Baccarat decanter. No one else was involved. After all, Victor's parents were dead and most of his friends were on the West Coast where he had been brought up. Mine were in Ohio."

"You felt isolated?"

"Oh, no. I had Victor. He was what mattered."

"And did he feel that you were what mattered?"

"If he hadn't I wouldn't have felt the way I did. I was so happy I didn't really feel married at all. I felt as if we were just playing at being married."

If she had expected sympathy, she had miscalculated. Dr. Sanders pounced. "Didn't it occur to you that you were

12

taking refuge in the idea of a play marriage because you were not happy at all at the deepest levels of the unconscious?"

"You do think of the most delightful questions, Dr. Sanders. No, it did not occur to me."

Dr. Sanders wrote something in his notebook and went on as blandly as ever. "The Victorians had a notion that there is a reaction after every marriage. Did you feel any such reaction?"

"No." From now on she would answer in monosyllables whenever she could. The less she said, the fewer weapons she gave him to use against her.

"Your mother died of cancer shortly after the wedding?"

"Yes."

"A little more detail, please."

"I don't want to talk about it."

"After your mother's death, your husband was transferred from New York to the Boston office of Luka, Incorporated. Do you miss New York?"

"No."

"Why don't you?"

"Boston is New York's nicest suburb if you can afford the shuttle flight. Just thirty minutes, half the time it takes to drive in from New Canaan."

"Why was your husband transferred?"

"I have no idea."

"A promotion?"

"How can I tell? I don't know anything about Luka, Incorporated. I don't really know what Victor does there. Something to do with mathematics, I think, but he never talks about it and I don't pry."

"Don't you think such reticence a little odd?"

13

"No. We had so many other things to talk about."

And yet . . . now she thought about it, there had been one odd thing about Victor's sudden transfer to Boston. It had changed him. Ever since the move he had seemed uneasy about something. Once or twice she had asked him if anything was wrong. Each time he had smiled and said, "No," but the smile was unconvincing.

It was only after the move to Boston that she found herself thinking sometimes: What kind of man have I married? What do I know about him?

The questions did not bother her because she was so happy in every other way.

Victor was the only human being she had ever known who really did love life for its own sake, no matter how rough the going or tragic the end. That was what had drawn her to him when they first met. All the small worries that used to nag a shy girl with a rather staid upbringing were blown away in his presence like cobwebs in a gust of fresh wind.

She had never expected to be loved by someone she loved. She knew such luck was rare and precarious. Death and change were always waiting in the wings. But she had learned from Victor himself to snatch happiness while it was there and never look too far behind or too far ahead.

She was used to earning a living and felt guilty when she didn't. Victor couldn't understand that. Did she need more money? She had only to ask him for it.

Even after a year of marriage she could not adjust to his large and lordly attitude toward money. Though his own parents had relatively little, he had been brought up in a family where there was a great deal, and the attitude had rubbed off on him. The founder of a fortune may be thrifty, but thrift is one thing he cannot pass on to his heirs of the

14

second and third generation. Victor automatically expected Scotland's best whiskey and Virginia's best tobacco, never a half-gallon of California "Burgundy-type" wine or the least expensive brand of cigarette. Sometimes Marina wondered if Victor's uneasiness could be financial, but . . .

Dr. Sanders' incisive voice cut across the flood of memories.

"Why did you choose Lincoln as a place to live?"

"Because it's the only place near Boston that looks more like backwoods than suburb. Lettice King found our house for us. She lives there herself between jobs."

"So you settled down in Lincoln and after a month or so you decided to give a housewarming. Do you remember what happened the day of the party?"

"I told you all that yesterday."

"I want to hear it again."

"No." Her voice throbbed. "Why do you always bear down on things that distress me?"

"For your own good, Marina." There was a glint in Dr. Sanders' eyes. Was he enjoying her distress?

She schooled her voice to sound as if she didn't care.

"It wasn't a big party. Just a few neighbors and some people from Victor's office in Boston and Lettice. I don't believe Victor likes Lettice much, but he was nice about asking her to the party. The only guest he really didn't want was his own cousin, Cornelius Skinner."

Again the film and sound track in her own mind began to unroll.

"I suppose we'll have to ask Cousin Cornelius and Anna," said Victor. "After all he is my boss."

"You don't really like him, do you?"

15

"I never have. He probably won't bother to come all the way from Connecticut, but we'll have to ask him. If we don't, he'll be mad."

"He sounds perfectly charming! What's his wife like?"

"Anna? She stays mad at everybody all the time."

"I can hardly wait . . ."

Dr. Sanders frowned as if he suspected there were things in her mind she was holding back.

He spoke softly. "Now we come to the accident."

"Must we go over that again?"

"How else can you hope to bring back your memory?"

"But I haven't forgotten anything!"

"Haven't you?" His smile was more unpleasant than his frown. "After concussion a patient usually forgets things that happened just before it."

"Don't you mean just after it?"

"No, before it. This is called retroactive amnesia. Memory comes back eventually, but it takes time and often therapy."

"You really believe there are things I've forgotten?"

"I know there are some things you have forgotten, and other things you think you remember which probably never happened. That's why you are here."

"How can you know what really happened?"

"There were other witnesses. I've talked to them. So now let me hear how much of the truth you remember today."

Had he any idea how much he was undermining her sense of reality?

A pulse pounded in her throat. A shortness of breath clenched her lungs. Her voice became thin and jerky.

"Victor came home from the office early that day. He seemed worried about something, but he didn't want to talk

16

about it. Just before the guests were due, we saw that we had no lemon peel. He wanted to run down to the grocer's for it, but I said I'd go. His job was keeping the fireplace from smoking."

"And then?"

"I took his car because it was standing in the drive-way."

"You had two cars?"

"Victor got me a little Italian car when I learned to drive. I was driving cautiously that day because I had only just got my license. It was a few minutes after sunset and I didn't switch on my headlights. Like all new drivers, I'd been studying my manual and I knew you weren't supposed to switch them on for another half hour.

"At the road I came to a full stop. I looked left. Nothing. I looked right. There was a car, white with a black top. I could see the silhouette of a man's head and shoulders inside. It was coming fast. I . . ."

She covered her face with both hands.

"Go on, Marina."

"I don't want to talk about it."

"You must face reality. What happened next?"

"I thought a bomb had gone off. There was nothing more until I woke up here and knew I had lost my baby."

"Marina, why do you insist on this fantasy?"

Her hands dropped from her face. "Fantasy?"

"There is no other word for it. None of these things happened. There was no other car. There was no pregnancy. What really happened? Had you been drinking? Was that why you hit the tree?"

Someone was screaming. Marina knew it was not she, for she never screamed.

17

She felt the sting of a needle in her arm.

As she passed into darkness, she heard the head nurse whisper:

"Do you think she believed you, Eric?"

Chapter Two

Was it the drug that floated her into an internal world where dreams are reality? Victor was lying beside her. She could feel his arms strong around her body, his lips on hers. Her passion was rising to meet his and then . . . nothing . . . no one there . . .

After a while the external world made itself felt through the most primitive sense, touch. Sheets were cool against her legs, a pillow smooth under one cheek.

Hearing came back more slowly, footfalls tiptoeing, voices hushed.

She opened her eyes. She was still in bed, lying on one side, facing a window. A dark shade cut off most of the view, but it was raised a few inches above the sill and the window was open. Through that narrow slit she could see the ripe gold of late afternoon sunshine. There were no bars at the window. That was a comfort.

"Awake, Mrs. Skinner?"

A young nurse, in white smock and slacks, stood beside the bed, holding a thermometer. It was cold against Marina's tongue. It tasted of disinfectant. The nurse took it out, glanced at it and shook it down without a word.

Now she was holding out one hand. On her palm lay a fat orange pill and a thin white one. Her other hand proffered water in a paper cup.

"What are those pills for?" asked Marina.

"The white's a sedative. The orange is an antibiotic."

"Why an antibiotic?"

"In cases of head injury we try to prevent infection before it develops. Any infection above the neck that gets out of hand may cause brain damage."

Marina swallowed the pills. "Did I suffer any other injuries besides the head injury?"

"Just a few scratches and bruises."

"Please tell me the whole truth. Did I have a miscarriage?"

"None is mentioned in your case history."

It was one thing to lose a baby. It was quite another to be told the baby had never existed.

"We'll call her Marina," Victor had said.

"No," she had answered. "We'll call him Victor."

They had bought things. A crib, sheets and blankets. Shirts almost small enough for a kitten. . . . Were all those memories just the sick fancies of a wounded mind?

Many nurses are impersonal. This one wasn't. There was compassion in her earnest brown eyes.

"I can't just call you 'Nurse.' What's your name?"

"Amelia Conrad."

"My friends call me Marina. Perhaps I ought not to ask you a question like this, but I've reached a point where I have to ask somebody. Why does Dr. Sanders hate me?"

Amelia dropped her eyes and began rearranging medicine bottles on the bedside table as if she needed something to do with her hands.

Shy, thought Marina. The way I used to be before I met Victor. Even if I never see him again, I'll never be the same person I was before I met him. . . .

Amelia found her voice. "Hate?" she repeated.

"It would be called hate in any other context. Whenever he discovers a question that upsets me, he bears down on it until I lose self-control. Are psychiatrists supposed to do that?"

Amelia answered without raising her eyes. "It's his version of a new technique called 'stress interview.' "

"A psychiatric third degree?"

"It might be hard to prove that it's ever been used to force a confession."

"But I have nothing to confess! Why can't I go home?"

"Have you told Dr. Sanders you want to go home?"

"I tell him every day, but he won't listen. I don't even know how long I've been here."

"Don't they let you see newspapers?"

"Yes, so I know today is June third but I don't know the day I came here. Dr. Sanders won't tell me."

"You came here the day of your accident, May thirty-first."

"I've been here three whole days? I can't believe it!"

At last Amelia lifted her eyes. "I'm probably breaking all sorts of rules to tell you this, but . . . do you know that a patient has a legal right to refuse medical treatment if he does not want it?"

"No, I didn't know."

"Legally, a doctor cannot keep you in a hospital or clinic against your will. Not unless he can prove to a judge that you are dangerous to yourself or others. Any doctor who tried it would be liable to a civil suit for false imprisonment. He

21

might even be charged with kidnapping."

"What can I do?"

"Don't just tell Dr. Sanders you want to go home. Insist on your legal right to do so. If he won't listen, appeal to your family."

"My only family is my husband. He hasn't been to see me, and Dr. Sanders won't let me telephone him."

"How can Dr. Sanders stop you? There are pay telephones in the hall on this floor."

"I didn't know that." Marina swung her legs out of bed and stood up. Everything seemed to tilt and spin. "I feel dizzy. Is it the sedative?"

"That's another thing. You don't have to swallow every pill they give you. You can always hold a pill in one cheek and spit it out later."

Marina slid her arms into the dressing gown Amelia was holding for her.

"Here are your bedroom slippers. You're going to need change. Take this."

She pushed a coin purse into Marina's pocket.

"But where's my own handbag?"

"Locked up in the registrar's safe with your watch and any other jewelry you had with you. That's routine with every patient who comes into the Sanders Clinic."

"How can I ever thank you?"

"Don't. I wouldn't be doing this unless I felt I had to. There comes a point when rules just don't matter."

"How can I reach you once I'm outside?"

"I live in Sudbury. I'm in the telephone book. Can you make it down the hall alone?"

"Aren't you coming with me?"

"You'll attract less attention alone. Lots of patients get

22

their exercise walking in the corridor. Try to look like one of them."

Marina had to walk slowly. Giddiness made her afraid of falling, the surest way to attract attention.

It took a conscious effort to steady her hand while she dialed the number of her own home. When ten rings brought no answer, she tried Victor's office number.

"Good morning!" The voice lilted with spurious cordiality. "This is Luka, Incorporated. How can we help you?"

"I wish to speak to Mr. Skinner. Victor Skinner."

"I am sorry, madam, but Mr. Skinner is in conference. If you would care to speak to his secretary and make an appointment, I can connect you."

"I'd like to speak to Mr. Skinner himself."

"I'm sorry, but—"

"This is Mrs. Skinner speaking."

"Oh . . ." A tiny ripple on the surface of the blandness. "I suppose he didn't have time to tell you."

"To tell me what?"

"He was called out of town rather suddenly this morning."

"Where is he?"

"In Rome at the moment."

"How can I reach him there?"

"You can't. He's just passing through Rome on his way to Teheran."

"But you just said he was in conference."

"The conference is in Teheran. I'm so sorry, Mrs. Skinner, but no doubt he'll call you when he gets there. Have a nice day!"

The telephone fell from Marina's hand.

She hardly knew how she got back to her room. When she could begin to think coherently again, she was back in bed, listening to the hum of an old-fashioned lawn mower outside the window. There was a summer smell in the air, fresh-cut grass stewing juicily in the sun's heat.

She could borrow more change from Amelia, but who else was there to call? She had never met Victor's boss, the Cousin Cornelius whom Victor did not like and who, she suspected, did not like Victor. Lettice King was in New York on a special assignment. She had not said whom she was working for or where she was staying and she would not be back until today or was it tomorrow?

Even if Marina could reach Cornelius or Lettice, would either of them believe her story?

I am being held in a private clinic against my will. I am not allowed to communicate with anybody outside. My psychiatrist is hostile to me and I don't know why. He tells me that I am remembering things that never happened.

Could anyone accept a story like that?

No one wanted to believe a doctor would abuse his power. The idea was too frightening. Yet it had happened.

In police states doctors were known to have declared dissenters insane so they could be imprisoned in mental hospitals for years. Could this happen outside police states?

Marina had read about one such case. Nearly a century ago a sane woman, the Belgian Princess Louise of Saxe-Coburg-Gotha, was confined in an Austrian mental hospital for years by a cuckolded husband who wanted revenge.

Psychiatrists signed reports saying that she had all the behavioral symptoms of brain damage. They were not quacks or crooks. One was the eminent doctor Baron von Krafft-Ebing.

Louise of Coburg finally escaped to a country beyond Austrian jurisdiction, but how many other cases like hers were unknown to history because the victim did not have friends outside to plan her escape for her?

If Marina was going to get out of this, she must make her own plan now and carry it out as soon as possible. . . .

Next afternoon a strange nurse came into the room with the two pills, white and orange. She was a languid ash-blonde.

"Where is the other nurse?" asked Marina.

"I don't know whom you mean."

"The one who was here at this time yesterday, Amelia Conrad."

"Oh, her. She's on vacation."

"When will she be back?"

"I dunno. Ready for your pills?"

This nurse was the brisk, impersonal kind.

"Don't keep me waiting. I do have other patients, you know."

"One question, please," said Marina. "Do you know when Nurse Conrad will be back?"

"It's hard to say. She has a pretty bad case of flu."

"I thought you said she was on vacation."

"Oh, no. She's ill."

The nurse popped a thermometer into Marina's mouth before she could ask any more questions.

After the nurse had gone, Marina got up and searched the room for a microphone. She didn't find any, but there must be one somewhere. How else explain the sudden disappearance of Nurse Conrad?

Walking no longer made her giddy. Was that because she had been holding the white pills in one cheek without swallowing them since yesterday? As soon as the nurses left the room she spat them out and flushed them down the drain.

Excitement kept her awake tonight, watching the hands of the little clock on her bedside table. They seemed motionless. She could not make herself believe they were moving unless she kept her eyes on a book from the clinic library for several minutes. Then, when she looked back at the clock again, she could see the hands had changed position.

When they reached midnight, she put her book aside and rose.

Once again the room seemed to reel, but this time it it was not drugs. It was fear.

She clung to a bedpost, eyes closed, until she felt steady. Then she stepped to the window, noiseless on her bare feet, and looked out.

Clouds. No stars. No moon. Perfect.

She dressed in trembling haste. She didn't brush her hair or cleanse her teeth. She left her nightgown where it fell on the floor.

She put her shoes under one arm and switched off the lights. Still noiseless, in stocking feet now, she felt her way to the door in the dark and eased it open a few inches.

To her right, the corridor turned a sharp angle. Beyond that corner, she could hear people whom she could not see. The office where night nurses kept watch was there. So were the elevators.

She prayed that no one would come around that corner in the next few minutes.

To her left, a longer stretch of corridor was empty. Doors on both sides led to rooms for patients. At this hour, they were all closed.

Was there no exit but the elevators?

Halfway down the left corridor a red neon tube was twisted into letters that spelled out the blessed words FIRE

STAIRS. That was what she had been hoping to see. Wherever there were elevators, there had to be fire stairs, and in well-planned buildings they were as far from the elevator shafts as possible.

She shut her own door behind her and tiptoed down the hall. She tried the door to the fire stairs. It yielded. It had to be unlocked. In case of fire there might not be time enough for anyone to rush around unlocking fire doors on every floor.

But what about the door at the bottom of the stairs?

She had to gamble on that.

She closed this door behind her so slowly there was no whisper of sound. She fled down the dim-lit stair silent as a bird on the wing.

The door at the bottom had one of those crossbars that must be depressed in order to open it.

She leaned on the bar. Nothing happened. Was it locked? She leaned harder and suddenly the door moved away from her.

A cool breath of outdoor air kissed her cheek. Leaves whispered overhead. One more step and she would be free.

A voice spoke out of the shadows.

"A good try, Marina, but it really won't do."

A whiff of cigar smoke came with him as he stepped from the shelter of the nearest tree. There was light enough from the house to see the concave face that was so close to caricature, but the light was too weak to show her the expression of his eyes.

"May I conduct you back to your room?"

"How did you know I would try to escape tonight?"

"I'm a chess player. Obviously it was your next move."

"Then why was this door at the bottom unlocked?"

"Did you ever hear of a Breton writer called Villiers de l'Isle-Adam? He wrote a story called 'The Torture of Hope.' It's about a prisoner of the Inquisition. His jailers deliberately leave the door of his cell unlocked so he will go through the agony of thinking he can escape, only to find in the end that he cannot. In the last war this little trick broke some prisoners when everything else failed. If I had told you escape was impossible, you might not have believed me. Now you know."

"I still don't believe you. There must be some way."

"No one has ever found any. I assure you, Marina, that no one has ever left this building without my permission."

"But there aren't even bars on the windows."

"Nor padded cells nor straitjackets. Such things are unnecessary since the invention of closed-circuit television and the discovery of drugs for the management of people.

"We do have to be watchful here because so many of our patients are alcoholics or drug addicts, but our vigilance is invisible. Concealed television screens monitor all corridors, and there is a silent alarm system switched on day and night. Every time the door of a a patient's room opens, a scanner flashes the room number on a viewing screen, and there are such screens on every floor. I left word with the nurse who was watching the screen on your floor to call me at once if your door was opened at any time tonight. While you were still on the fire stairs, I was coming down more quickly in the elevator."

"And I suppose there's a microphone in my room?"

"How did you guess?"

When she didn't answer, he answered for her. "Oh, I see. Amelia Conrad."

"I haven't the slightest idea what you're talking about."

28

"Haven't you?" He was amused. "Don't worry about Amelia. She's perfectly well. How could you possibly think otherwise?"

"Dr. Sanders."

"Yes, Marina?"

Now that he knew she disliked his use of her first name, he used it incessantly.

She plowed on. "How long am I to stay here?"

"Until you are restored to health."

"When will that be?"

"How can I possibly say? That depends on you."

"Who decides when I am well?"

"I do."

"What is the matter with me?"

"Haven't I made that clear? I'm sorry. You had a severe concussion with retroactive amnesia, followed by something more serious: gross delusions of memory. I suspect brain damage."

"I don't believe that is why you are keeping me here."

"Don't you?"

"I'm sure you have no legal right to detain me against my will. Not unless you can prove that I am dangerous to myself or others

"Do you really think that would be difficult?"

Nothing could disturb his equanimity. He even smiled as he left her at the door of her room.

She lay down on her bed, but it was a long time before she fell asleep.

There must be some way to get out of this place and she was going to find it . . .

Chapter Three

The duel between Marina and Dr. Sanders was becoming more deadly. He promised that he would try to get Victor for her on the telephone, but he was singularly unsuccessful in all his attempts to do so. Victor could not have seemed more remote if he had been on another planet.

Yet Marina needed him as she had never needed him before. He was the only other witness to the accident. He had been standing at the head of the driveway when it happened. He must have seen the the other car. He might even have seen the other driver. He was the only person in the world who might be able to restore her faith in her own sanity now.

Dr. Sanders pointed out that Iran was a foreign country incompletely industrialized and on the other side of the world. Linguistic problems and mechanical breakdowns were to be expected when telephoning there.

"But the head office of Luka must be able to reach their own office in Teheran!" protested Marina.

"Not in the last day or so," returned Dr. Sanders. "I've asked them for help and they've promised to let me know as soon as they do get through."

Marina herself had secretly borrowed enough change from one of the other nurses to initiate several collect calls to Victor at the Teheran office. The one time she was able to get through, a voice said that Victor wasn't there at the moment. Before she could leave a message for him, she was cut off. She was never able to get through again.

The next time Dr. Sanders appeared in Marina's room she tried something new. She made a point of agreeing with everything he said. Yes, she had hit a tree because she had been drinking. No, there was no other car involved. Pregnancy? What was he talking about? She had never been pregnant.

At last she had surprised him. There were signs he could not quite control—a tiny flicker of his eyelids, a sudden check in his fluent speech, a growing irritation he could not keep out of his eyes.

What would he do now?

It was three days before she found out.

"Marina, I must congratulate you on your remarkable recovery."

"So there was no brain damage after all?"

"Apparently not."

"So I can go home?"

"Perhaps. Why not?"

Now he had surprised her. Was it really going to be that easy?

Or was this just the torture of hope again?

The things that human beings do to one another make the way of a cat with a mouse or the way of a dog with a cat seem innocent. There is no intent in such animal behavior, just Lorenz' inherited response mechanism, but there is always intent in man. He is the only animal who knows that he must die, the only animal who understands that he has a father, and the only animal who realizes what he is doing when he is being cruel.

Marina had hoped to force Dr. Sanders' hand, but she had not expected him to surrender in three days.

She tried to smother anxiety. I am going home. I am going to see Victor. Everything is going to be all right.

But she didn't really believe it.

The nurses kept urging her to walk about the grounds.

"You should exercise every day before you go home, Mrs. Skinner. You've been in bed so long it's lowered your muscle tone."

The walks did make her feel stronger physically, but the anxiety was still there. She had a queasy feeling that somehow, at the very last moment, Dr. Sanders would find a way to prevent her leaving after all.

He surprised her again the next morning when he said: "Good news, Marina! You are going home tomorrow."

"Is Victor back?"

"Yes, he's going to pick you up here tomorrow after luncheon."

"Can I talk to him on the telephone now?"

"I'm afraid not. He's in New York today, but I have no idea just where. There's not much point in trying to find him now when you're going to see him tomorrow anyway."

She didn't argue. She knew she could never make Dr. Sanders understand how much she longed for the sound of Victor's voice.

When the great day came, the nurses helped her pack her bag and brought her the envelope that contained her money, watch and rings from the registrar's safe.

She was too restless to sit quietly in her room before

luncheon. She went downstairs for a last walk about the grounds.

She had a favorite seat there now, a wrought-iron chair close to a retaining wall that reinforced the bank of a high, grassy terrace. On clear days the stone wall radiated the sun's warmth to anyone sitting in the chair. Today it happened to be cloudy, but habit took her to the chair the way a kitten will snuggle up to a cold radiator when central heating is turned off in summer.

She had hardly settled herself on the seat cushions when she heard voices on the terrace twenty feet above.

"So you're letting Marina Skinner go?"

It was the voice of the head nurse.

"Am I?" That was Dr. Sanders.

Marina was so close to the wall they they could not see her unless they came to the edge of the terrace and looked down. Where they were standing, farther back, they could have no idea that there was anyone below.

The familiar tone between them did not surprise her. She had known they were lovers the first time she saw them together.

"But the floor nurse said—"

"The floor nurse knows nothing about it," retorted Sanders. "Marina Skinner thinks she is going home, but I have a feeling she will be here for a long time to come."

"Eric, what are you doing?"

"I'm not doing anything. Marina is going to do something herself. I shall simply give her opportunities."

"What is she going to do?"

"I can't foresee details, but I am sure she will demonstrate somehow that she is totally unfit to leave this clinic."

"I suppose you'll take advantage of some little slip that

you would overlook in anyone else. Why do you hate her so?"

"My dear Jane, a psychiatrist doesn't hate his patients."

"Doesn't he?" The head nurse laughed.

There could be no sound of footfalls on that velvet turf, but the sound of voices was receding. Marina waited until there were no sounds at all before she walked back to the house.

She did not go into the dining room where ambulatory patients took their meals. She had no appetite for luncheon now. She went upstairs to her own room and tried to read the daily newspaper, but she could not get beyond the headlines with their bloody little wars and their squalid little scandals.

She had repudiated all the things that Dr. Sanders regarded as her delusions. How could he make her deviate from that line now? Or was this going to be a new delusion?

The floor nurse came in to ask her if she was ready.

Marina managed a smile.

"Quite ready, thank you."

They both heard footfalls outside the door.

The nurse smiled back at her. "That must be your husband now."

Marina's heart began to labor thickly as if her blood had turned to clay.

She struggled to her feet. "Victor . . ."

But it was Dr. Sanders who came into the room first.

His mood was jovial.

"Good morning, my dear Marina. Or, rather, good afternoon. Here is someone you have wanted to see for a long time. Come in, Mr. Skinner."

A tall young man stood on the threshold. He carried his

34

height without awkwardness. There was a smile in his dark eyes and his voice was warm.

"Marina, darling . . ."

There was only one thing wrong with him.

He wasn't Victor.

II - OUTSIDE

II OUTSIDE

Chapter Four

The flow of time seemed to pause for a moment. Shock forced a crowd of conflicting responses into her mind where they all jostled and blocked one another.

This man is not my husband.

Before she could say the words, she could hear Dr. Sanders inevitable retort:

Don't you even know your own husband, Marina? I'm afraid we shall have to keep you here indefinitely. . . .

She looked at the impostor again. Height, weight, build and coloring were Victor's. Could she be mistaken? Was this Victor?

He was returning her look, eyes bright with something she could not identify. Curiosity? Challenge?

She took a deep breath.

"Victor, darling, I've missed you so much!"

She threw both arms around his neck and kissed him.

His response was cold and confused.

Victor would never respond to anybody's kiss that way.

This man didn't even speak to her now.

He spoke to Dr. Sanders. "I must thank you for all you

have done for my wife. And you, too." He spared a glance for the head nurse. "But now I must take her home. Is this bag her only luggage? Come, Marina."

Numb and silent she walked with him down the corridor, into the elevator, across the lobby.

Only when they came to the parking lot did she break out of her trance.

"That's my car. The blue Fiat Victor gave me when I learned to drive."

"Of course. You smashed up my car. Remember?"

"You mean I smashed up Victor's car. Where is it now?"

"In the body shop near the station. I took my car there myself."

"So all traces of collision with another car could be removed?"

He held the door open. She slid into the passenger seat. He got in beside her and the car moved out of the lot onto the county road. At last they were in a place where no one could watch them or overhear what they said.

"Well?" She tried to make her voice cool and firm. "Where is Victor and who are you?"

He took his eyes off the road for a moment to glance at her. "I am Victor Skinner."

"And I suppose that now you're going to tell me all about your interesting trip to Iran? Please don't bother. We both know perfectly well you're not Victor."

"You have just acknowledged me as Victor publicly."

"I had to. It was the only way to get out of there when Dr. Sanders was so hostile to me. Where are we going now?"

"Home to Lincoln. Where else would I take my devoted little wife?"

"That isn't funny. Have you no idea how worried I am

about Victor? You just make it worse when you pretend you are he. We both know you're not."

For a moment he concentrated on entering the stream of traffic on the turnpike. She took the opportunity to study him more closely. Like Victor, he was relaxed and easy, a man most women would find attractive. Unlike Victor, his jaw looked stubborn and and there was no spark of humor in his eyes. She thought he would be a dull companion for any length of time, and she could not help feeling sorry for any woman fool enough to marry him.

There was an air of muted prosperity about him that she did not associate with crooks. The Swiss watch on his wrist was so plain you hardly noticed its quality. His clothes were cut artfully from fine materials, but so neutral in color and simple in style that he would pass unnoticed in a crowd.

When he settled down in the middle lane, she spoke again.

"Was Dr. Sanders surprised when I accepted you as Victor?"

"How could he be surprised? He had never seen Victor Skinner and he had never seen me, so he expected you to accept me as Victor."

"So now you admit you're not Victor?"

"I'm tired of arguing."

They were leaving the turnpike. Whoever he was, he was well briefed. He knew these roads. He didn't hesitate for a moment to take the one that led to her house, though the misleading road sign said BOSTON.

"What makes you think Dr. Sanders is hostile to you?"

She told him.

"Everything the man said to me was a lie. I know I was pregnant. I know there was another car. I saw it."

"Did you see the driver?"

41

"Only just. I wouldn't recognize him again. He was simply a silhouette, a man's head and shoulders against the light. The sun was setting behind him."

"Why should Dr. Sanders lie about things like that? What does he get out of it?"

"I don't know, but he must have some reason for it. Obviously he wanted to keep me in the clinic indefinitely, and he could only do that by making me believe I'd lost my mind. The whole thing must have something to do with Victor's disappearance."

"Are you sure Victor has disappeared?"

"No one seems to know where he is, including his own office, and . . . Wait a minute! You must be sure he has disappeared or you would never have dared to pose as Victor. You would have been too afraid he might walk in on you at any moment. What do you know about this?"

He didn't answer. He just stopped the car beside the Skinner mailbox and said:

"Why don't you look inside?"

She looked, but there were no letters.

"That's odd. We usually get something every day even if it's only junk mail."

The man beside her was looking up the driveway.

Her gaze followed his through trees to the house at the top of the hill.

What is sadder than an empty house where you have once been happy?

Already weeds were taking over. Dull light from a gray sky did not help. With every shutter closed, the place looked as if it had been deserted for years.

"Is this where the accident happened?" he asked her.

"Yes. That's the tree I hit. You can see the trunk is scarred."

From here it was obvious that anyone standing at the top of the driveway must have seen the accident in the road below. That was where Victor had been standing when she left the house. She had glanced back once, just a moment before the accident. He was still there. He must have seen what happened.

The impostor stopped his car at the open space in front of the house.

She hung back to see if he had a key to the front door.

He did, and once inside, he moved as confidently as if he had been in his own house, down the hall to the living room overlooking the garden.

Marina was aware of dust everywhere. The air smelled stale as if no window had been opened for a long time.

Yet, strangely, the living room looked as if Victor had just left it a moment ago. There was an empty glass on the table near his favorite chair. Beside it lay the latest issue of the *Bulletin of the Atomic Scientists*. It was open at an article about the use of lasers in eye operations.

Marina dropped into the first chair she came to, leaning her head against the high back, resting her hands on the arms.

"I am going to the police."

"They'll never accept your story."

"Why not?"

"You're asking them to believe that Dr. Sanders is a crook. They can't accept that. They know a man in his position doesn't need to turn crook. He can get everything he wants legitimately."

"Can he? Doesn't that depend on what he wants?"

"Look at it this way. He told you he was a chess player. Do you think any chess player would fail to anticipate a move as obvious as going to the police now? If you do, it's your word against his. You're suffering from a head injury. He has the whole staff of the clinic to back him up. The only witness you might call is your husband and he has disappeared. You haven't a chance of getting anyone to believe your story and I'm sure Dr. Sanders realizes that. He planned it that way."

Marina felt that sudden slide in the pit of the stomach that is the most unpleasant symptom of fear.

She could not afford to lose her nerve. She answered him without hesitation. "Why is it you don't want me to go to the police? You must have some reason."

He didn't answer her question. He went on as if she had not spoken at all.

"Have you thought how your life will change if you go to the police? Your name is Skinner now. Your husband is Cornelius Skinner's first cousin. Everyone has heard of Skinner Industries. Anything that happens to you is news. Do you want to go through the ordeal of trial by newspaper and television with your name and picture everywhere? For you'll be on trial in the newspapers no matter what happens or doesn't happen in court.

"Think of the nasty public speculations about your private life. Think of the innuendos that will be more widely spread every time you deny them. Think of the days you'll have to spend hiding from photographers. You may even have to hire bodyguards.

"We live in a curious culture today. Everyone wants money and notoriety, but everyone hates the few who actu-

44

ally get money and notoriety. They immediately become the targets of envy and malice. People watch them for the first sign of weakness the way vultures watch a dying animal. Do you want that?"

"I want to find Victor. That's more important. He must be in trouble. Nothing else would keep him away from me like this. But you've given me an idea. If the Skinners are all that important, why can't I approach the police through Cornelius Skinner?"

"That's the most ridiculous idea I ever heard."

"Why? If I have Skinner Industries behind me, all the power won't be on Dr. Sanders' side. I haven't met Cornelius, but he is Victor's first cousin and he knows who I am. If he doesn't know Victor has disappeared, someone should tell him."

"If you insist on anything so foolish . . ." He interrupted himself. "What was that?"

"I didn't hear anything."

"I did. Someone's outside."

He rose, then paused. "Don't look so woebegone. Trust me."

"Why should I? You haven't told me a thing about yourself. Not even your name. Who are you?"

"Wait here. I'll be back in a minute."

He shut the door behind him as he left the room. She could hear nothing but the ticking of an old carriage clock on the chimney piece and a trill of notes from some bird outside the closed windows.

She had forgotten they were closed.

She rose to open one. The bird was quiet now, and she was too far from the fireplace to hear the clock.

She could stand the silence just so long.

Then she opened the door into the hall.

It was empty.

She ran to the front door and threw it open.

There was no sign of the impostor, but her car was still standing in the driveway.

Would she ever be able to drive it again?

She went into the house. The telephone was in a cubbyhole under the stairs. Last Christmas she had given Victor a little green leather book for unlisted numbers. It was still there.

She found the number she wanted under the letter "C" and dialed the operator.

"This is a person-to-person call to Greenwich, Connecticut. I want to speak to Cornelius Skinner."

Chapter Five

Skinner Industries had its largest plant investments near Boston and New York, so it was only natural that Cornelius Skinner should have a residence between the two cities in Connecticut.

If you own and run a multinational corporation, you have no home, just residences scattered all over the world. There were penthouses on top of Skinner skyscrapers in Manhattan and Hong Kong. There were Skinner ranches in Wyoming and Venezuela. There was a smart, modern town house in Hyde Park Square and a fragile, faded *hôtel particulier* in the rue de Bellechasse. There were villas in Morocco and Costa Rica, where extradition laws are comfortable, and, for roughing it "democratically," a camp in western Canada a hundred miles north of Georgian Bay.

If Cornelius wearied of beaches, there were always mountains, and if he tired of both, there were always cities. He could arrive at any one of his places without even a toothbrush and find everything he needed for daily living ready and waiting for him. As he often said, it saved hotel bills.

But Greenwich was where he spent most of his time. The

house stood in four hundred acres of woodland that included half a mile of beach. He relied on the fact that it was well hidden for his security. The address and telephone number were not listed anywhere. A wilderness of trees and underbrush hid the private road from the public road. Other trees and shrubbery had been planted to hide the house from the water. If there was an alarm system, it was like the one at the Sanders Clinic, invisible and inaudible, operating with signal light.

The entrance was artfully unpretentious. No name was posted. Just a simple, five-barred gate that anyone could open. There was a gatehouse, but it was modest and the gatekeeper was not a guard, just a hobbling, old pensioner without a gun or even a dog.

The private road was unpaved. It would be muddy in spring, dusty in summer and always uninviting.

Marina was glad she had telephoned before she set out. Now she had only to show the gatekeeper her driver's license and he waved her on with a smile.

The house itself surprised her with its charm. It was a Norman farmhouse in miniature. Of course, there was no sign of the manure piles and compost heaps that come with the real thing, but it did have the graceful windows, slate roof and hand-molded bricks of Normandy. The bricks were whitewashed and the shutters were painted a rich black. Against this chaste background, the flower beds were a riot of color, guarded by chubby, smiling *amorini,* cast in lead, obvious old and probably Venetian. It was a little jewel box of a house, and later Marina was to learn that Cornelius had taken a leaf from the younger brother of Louis XVI and called the place modestly, or coyly, Bagatelle.

The door was opened by a matronly, pink-faced woman in

summer white. Through the doorway Marina could see straight through French windows in the opposite wall to the waters of the sound, almost as blue as the Caribbean in the spring sunshine.

"Mrs. Victor Skinner," she said. "I made an appointment by telephone through a secretary to see Mr. Skinner this afternoon."

"Be pleased to enter, madam." The speech had a foreign flavor, but Marina could not place the nationality. Dutch? Scandinavian?

She was ushered into a double drawing room. A gesture indicated a chair, delicately carved and gilded, as Venetian as the *amorini.*

"Would madam care for refreshments while she waits?"

"No, thank you."

The door closed without a sound. The absence of noise was one of many luxuries people took for granted in a house like this.

The room was blond. The Aubusson rugs were chosen for their soft hues as well as their quality and antiquity. The dominant color of curtains and cushions was somewhere between white jade and champagne. Here and there a higher note was struck: the sunny blue of Monet's lily ponds or the blush rose of a Kwan Yin carved in quartz and polished to a soft glow.

"Well? What do you want?"

Marina started to her feet. She had not been looking toward the door and she had not heard anyone come into the room, but now, standing before her, was a small, swarthy woman with a monkey's face and angry eyes.

Her tweeds were hairy and shabby. If you had seen her in a supermarket with a shopping bag over one arm, you would

49

have thought her a suburban housewife who had never been able to afford any of the things she really wanted.

"I asked for Mr. Skinner," said Marina.

"I know you did, but he's much too busy to see anyone this afternoon. I'm his wife, Anna, and I suppose you're Victor's wife, Marina. I can't imagine why you came here today. Is it really urgent?"

"Oh, yes."

"If it's financial, there's nothing we can do to help you."

"It isn't."

"If it's personal, we're not interested. We didn't want Victor to marry you in the first place. If you and he are unhappy now, you'll just have to work out your own problems as best you can."

"It's nothing like that. Victor has disappeared."

"Nonsense! He's in Iran on a mission for one of the Skinner companies, Luka, Incorporated. A very delicate mission."

"Are you sure he's in Iran now?"

"What makes you think he isn't?"

"I've been trying to reach him there by telephone, but he's never in the Teheran office, and they don't seem to have any idea where he is or when he will be back."

"You must be exaggerating."

"Truly, I'm not. I was in a car accident just before he left and—"

"I read all about that in the newspapers. Don't tell me you drove yourself here today so soon afterward."

"If I didn't make myself drive now, I'd never drive again."

"How long were you in that Sanders Clinic?"

"About a week. Dr. Sanders only let me go this morning because he thought Victor was back in this country, but he

50

isn't. No one can tell me where he is."

"Is that all?"

"I'd much rather discuss this with your husband. I think it must have something to do with Skinner Industries."

"And you think I am unfamiliar with the management of Skinner Industries? The corporation was founded with my money when I married Cornelius. I have had a finger in every pie ever since. Why not tell me?"

"Because I doubt if you would believe me."

"And you think Cornelius is more credulous?"

Marina picked her next words carefully. "Of course not. But I think he may have a little more experience in the way things can go wrong in big organizations."

"Oh, you think so, do you? My dear good girl, whether you talk to me or not is a matter of total indifference to me, but you cannot talk to my husband this afternoon. He has far more important things to do than listen to a young woman just out of a psychiatric clinic whose only claim on his attention is the unfortunate circumstance that one of his cousins was fool enough to marry her."

Marina began to laugh. She couldn't help it.

Anna's eyes blazed. "If you think what I say is funny, I must beg you to excuse me."

"I'm sorry, but I'm so worried about Victor that I hardly know what I'm doing. You and your husband are the only people to whom I can turn for help. I have no family of my own. I'm quite alone."

Anna was halfway to the door. She stopped and turned to give Marina a long, hard look.

"As bad as that? Then we'd better go into the study. There's no privacy here."

She led the way through the second drawing room to a

single door and knocked. When no one answered, she opened the door and beckoned Marina to follow her into the room beyond.

It was smaller than the other rooms, and furnished like a scholar's working library, with three walls of books. One of them was interrupted by a fireplace where a small wood fire was dying. The fourth wall was filled largely with French windows opening onto a terrace.

Anna closed the door and sat down behind a desk, waving Marina to a chair opposite.

"Now tell me everything."

Marina looked down at her own hands, clenched and rigid in her lap. "I wasn't happy in the clinic, but they wouldn't let me go home. That frightened me so much I tried to escape one night, but Dr. Sanders stopped me."

"Are you asking me to believe that the Sanders Clinic held you a prisoner against your will?"

"Indeed they did. I was beginning to wonder if they would ever let me go, when quite suddenly Dr. Sanders reversed himself. He said that Victor was coming to pick me up, but the man who came for me wasn't Victor. He was a total stranger."

"How did this Dr. Sanders react when you told him the man wasn't Victor?"

"I didn't tell him. Don't you understand? I had reached a point where I would have done anything to get out of the Sanders Clinic. I pretended to accept the stranger as Victor so I could walk out with him."

"Who was this stranger? And what became of him?"

"I have no idea. We had no real chance to talk. He disappeared almost as soon as we got home. I don't know why."

"And what has all this to do with Skinner Industries?"

"I don't know, but is it coincidence that Victor disappeared on a trip to Iran for Skinner Industries and all these things happened to me at the same time?"

"Why don't you go to the police?"

"They wouldn't take me any more seriously than you do. I have only one hope. If Cousin Cornelius will put his influence behind my story, the police will listen to him. Is it too much to ask? After all, Victor is his cousin and works for him."

"Have you fully considered the possibility that all these things you say happened at the clinic may be sheer delusion caused by concussion after your accident?"

"That's what Dr. Sanders kept implying, but I know he's wrong."

"Mistaken or lying?"

"I don't know."

"What motive would he have for lying?"

"That's one of the things I must find out. Won't you help me?"

"No. Neither Cornelius nor I will have anything to do with this situation. It's your affair and Victor's, not ours. Poor boy! He always was absurdly susceptible to young women, but until you came along he managed to stay out of trouble."

"Was I trouble?"

"From our point of view, yes. We knew nothing about you, and Victor happens to have access to all sorts of classified information at Luka. I never told Cornelius, but when you became engaged to Victor I put private detectives on your trail to find out as much as I could about your past. When they didn't come up with anything criminal, I let Victor go ahead and marry you without further protest. After all, if it hadn't been you, it would probably have been someone else just as ineligible or worse."

"I would not have come to you for help if I had known that."

Daylight was waning. Anna lit a desk lamp and went on as if she had not heard.

"I doubt if Victor's in real trouble now. He'll probably come bouncing back someday when you least expect him, providing, of course, that he isn't seriously involved with some other woman. If he is, he'll want a divorce. Have you thought of that?"

"No. We've been married just a year . . ."

"So many brides still have illusions about the first year. Actually there are lots of psychiatric case histories about husbands who stray during the first year and even the first month. Better think that over before you open Pandora's box by going to the police. . . . And now you really will have to excuse me. It's nearly dinnertime."

Anna's finger was reaching for a bell button inlaid on the top of the desk.

Marina rose. "Don't bother to ring. I can find my own way out."

She was almost at the door when a quick step sounded on the terrace outside the French windows, and a man stepped into the room.

"Anna, what's going on here?"

This had to be Cousin Cornelius. Marina was surprised to see that he was small and frail, almost dwarfish. Only his head was large. His slender neck drooped under its weight. Perhaps if was this that made his shoulders so stooped and round. There was no actual hump, but his posture gave the same impression as a hunchback, and even the eyes, behind

54

thick lenses, had the wounded look of a cripple's eyes.

The most attractive things about him were his hands and his voice. The hands were narrow and shapely. The voice was low and unhurried.

"Is something wrong?"

Anna moistened her lips with the pale tip of a coated tongue.

"Nothing that need concern you, Cornelius."

"Everything that happens in this house concerns me." His voice lost none of its calmness but it was firm as granite. "Who is this young lady? Please present me."

"Victor's wife, Marina."

"Oh?" The sad eyes moved in Marina's direction. "How do you do, my dear? I am happy to see you here at last. Welcome to Bagatelle!"

After Anna's harshness it was difficult for Marina to respond to Cornelius adequately, but she managed to say: "I'm glad to be here."

"Now sit down and tell me what's wrong. There is something wrong, isn't there?"

He was smiling as he held an armchair for her.

"I don't know where Victor is. I'm afraid something has happened to him."

"What kind of thing?"

"Cornelius!"

"Yes, Anna?"

"I really don't believe this is wise."

"Don't you?" The smile left his face. Where he was standing, lamplight struck the thick lenses of his glasses brilliantly. It was impossible to see his eyes behind the glitter, but his voice was still calm. "Didn't you tell me a little while ago that you had a headache?"

"Yes, Cornelius, but—"

"I think, my dear, that you need a little rest. Why don't you go upstairs now and lie down so you will feel better by dinnertime?"

"I am not tired."

"It would be advisable."

"Very well, Cornelius. Good night, Cousin Marina."

"Oh, but you're going to see her again this evening." He turned to Marina. "You will stay to dinner, won't you?"

She longed to refuse, but how could she turn down her first chance to get real help for Victor?

"You're very kind, but isn't it inconvenient at such short notice?"

"It is not inconvenient at all, is it, Anna?"

"Oh, not in the least. I am delighted."

Anna would have thought it ill-bred to slam the door, but she did close it with an audible snap.

Cornelius sighed. "Care for a glass of sherry?"

"Oh, yes, please!"

He opened a Chinese cabinet that stood between two of the windows and brought out a decanter and glasses.

Marina took a healthy swallow. She needed it.

Cornelius took only the slightest sip, then set his glass down beside hers on the desk.

"Now tell me, and don't hold anything back. Talk as if I were a tape recorder. . . . That's an idea. Do you mind if I make a tape of this?"

"Of course not. Then, after it's typed, I can read over what I've said and catch any mistakes."

"Just what I thought." He pulled open the bottom drawer of the desk. A recorder was already there, spools in place, tape threaded. All he had to do was switch it on.

He leaned back in his chair, smiling.

"Ready?"

She began to talk, hesitantly at first. When she saw him turn up the volume, she took a grip on herself, trying to speak more loudly and clearly with her lips closer to the microphone.

It was an hour's spool, but in less than half an hour she had said everything she wanted to say. As an assistant editor at *Home Exquisite* she had learned to condense a text without losing clarity, and apparently she had not lost the knack.

"Well?" she said when she had finished. "Do you believe any of that?"

"I believe all of it." He hesitated, then seemed to come to a decision. "I am afraid I have bad news for you. This is something Anna does not know. I have been trying to find Victor for two weeks, the same two weeks you were in the clinic."

"What happened?"

"We don't know. No one at Luka has had any word from Victor since he took off for Iran. We gave out a story that he was in Teheran to keep people from talking. Actually, we have no idea where he is or what he is doing."

"And you haven't told the police?"

"Victor was last seen in Rome. In these international situations I prefer to rely largely on our own security officers. They work with Italian or Iranian police when it is productive, but in this case I judged it would be counterproductive."

"Why?"

"Foreign police have been known to leak information to American newspapermen who make far too much of trifling incidents and then call it freedom of the press. We can rely on the discretion of our own security officers."

"Did you never think of letting me know what was going on?"

"Of course I did. When I read in the newspapers that you had been taken to the Sanders Clinic after your accident, I tried to reach you there by telephone. Dr. Sanders said you had had a complete breakdown and must not be disturbed. I had no reason to distrust Dr. Sanders then."

"And now?"

"Now it's quite a different matter. One of my secretaries will type this while we're at dinner."

Marina had not noticed the voice box on the desk until now when Cornelius flipped a switch and spoke into it.

"Miss Atkins?"

"Yes, Mr. Skinner."

"I'm leaving an hour tape on my desk. I'd like a ribbon copy and two Xeroxes in a couple of hours. Can do?"

"Oh, yes, Mr. Skinner."

Marina deduced that this secretary was elderly. A young secretary would be addressed in the modern style as "Susie" or "Betsy" or "Peggy," though she would still call him "Mr. Skinner."

Cornelius reversed the switch and turned back to Marina. "One Xerox for you to take home with you and one for my files. I'll see that the ribbon copy gets to the right people the first thing tomorrow."

"Who are the right people?"

"I vote in Connecticut, but Luka is incorporated in Massachusetts and its head office is there. As president of Luka, Incorporated, I shall take the matter up with the governor, who happens to be a personal friend of mine. If he sends it on to the attorney general's office, I am sure they will give it their prompt attention. More sherry? No? Then let's see if

Anna has come downstairs yet."

They found her in the double drawing room. She had changed into crimson silk brocade that covered her from chin to wrist and swept the floor. The pearls in her choker were as fat as lima beans. Their luster had the depth found only in the real pearl with its extra layers of invisible faceting.

Yet all this did nothing for her appearance. She was still a small, swarthy woman with a monkey's face and angry eyes.

At table Cornelius addressed himself to both women impartially, but Marina was the one who usually responded. Only twice did Anna even bother to contradict her husband.

The first time was when Cornelius suggested that the climate of New England was changing. She promptly reeled off meteorological statistics to show that this was not so. The second time was when Cornelius said that most divorces were caused by infidelity. Anna announced that no matter what anyone said in court, the real cause of all divorces was boredom.

"It would be quite impossible for me to endure a husband who bored me," she said looking steadily at Cornelius.

Even he had run out of small talk by the time they went into the double drawing room for coffee.

Desperately Marina looked around the room for some conversation piece and settled on a portrait over one of the two fireplaces at either end of the long room.

"What a beautiful boy!"

"My son, Thereon." Anna rose to switch on a light below the picture frame. It brought out every detail of a fresh, young face with dark, brilliant eyes. He was wearing a lemon-yellow sport shirt with open neck and rolled-up sleeves. The artist had painted head and torso only, setting them against a background of cloudy gray that might have been sky, though there was no landscape in view. The boy did not look more than twenty.

The proper thing to say was: "He looks like both of you," but Marina could not bring herself to say it.

"He looks like a poet," she ventured at last.

"He is a genius." Anna spoke as she might have said: He is a student, or he is a tennis player.

Cornelius intervened, tactful as always. "Anna means that the boy has total recall. He can solve arithmetical problems instantly without a pocket calculator or pencil and paper. If you ask him the cube root of some long number or the weekday of the Battle of Marathon, he'll give you the answer in seconds as if he were a living computer, but he does not know how he does it.

"He is not a genius. He is an ordinary boy with uncanny gifts. If he had not managed to scrape through two years at Harvard, I would say he is what the French call a *savant idiot.*"

"You know I detest that expression *savant idiot,*" said Anna. "There is nothing subnormal about Thereon."

Marina tried to distract her from another clash with her husband by asking where the boy was now.

It was a mistake.

"I neither know nor care." She spoke with concentrated bitterness. "He's what they call a dropout. He left Harvard in his junior year. He doesn't even have a job. He has nothing." She switched off the light under the picture. "Cornelius, I still have a headache."

"I'm so sorry."

"It doesn't matter." She brushed away sympathy as if it were an irritant. "But I think I'd better go back to bed. Don't

60

worry about Victor, Marina. He's not worth it. His parents spoiled him. He never bothered to write his mother when he was away at school."

"He was considerably younger then," said Cornelius. "And he wasn't married or employed by Skinner Industries. I'm beginning to worry about him."

"Well, I'm not. I'm sure he'll turn up in a day or so, totally unrepentant and enormously pleased with himself as usual. Good night, Marina."

Cornelius opened a door for her and she swept out of the room.

"I'm sorry I asked about Thereon," said Marina. "I didn't realize—"

"That's all right. I know where he is. He's living in an old house in Brookline with some other irresponsibles his own age. I haven't told his mother because I don't want her to bother him. She can't forgive him for what he calls his 'anticulture life-style.' She had such high hopes for him once. . . . Shall we look at those scripts now?"

"Oh, yes."

Cornelius touched a bell. Typescript and Xerox were neatly stapled in pale blue covers. The typing was immaculate. Marina saw one or two places that could have been made even more concise, but she couldn't bear to tamper with anything so flawless.

"More coffee?"

"Thank you." She drank it quickly and put down the little cup and saucer. "I really must go now and I don't quite know how to thank you for listening to me. I had reached a point where I just did not know what to do."

"Your responsibility is ended now, child," said Cornelius. "Go home and get a good night's rest. The whole thing will probably turn out to be something quite simple and unimportant after all. As soon as Victor gets back, bring him to dinner. Then we can all have a good laugh at this silly business together. Where did you leave your car?"

"In the front driveway."

He went out to the car with her. A lamp above the front door flooded the sweep of gravel. He leaned through the car window to drop a light, cousinly kiss on her cheek.

"After what you've been through, I don't have to tell you to drive carefully!"

He stepped back as the engine came to life. She turned the car around, then stopped to look back. He was standing on the low steps that led to the front door now. She waved and he waved back at her. The car followed its own lights through the dark tunnel made by the shrubbery that grew on either side of the driveway.

She was almost at the public road when realization struck her. She had forgotten the Xerox of her typed tape recording.

Should she call him tomorrow and ask him to mail it to her? A pity to put him to that trouble when it would be so much easier for both of them if she went back and picked up the Xerox now. A little awkward after all those good-byes, still less bother for everybody.

She turned the car back the way she had just come.

When she reached the house again the lamp no longer shone above the front door. The whole façade was in darkness. Had everybody gone to bed already?

No, there was light on the grass at the side of the house coming from the back. Cornelius must have returned to the study.

Wouldn't it be better to tap on his window there than to rouse the whole household by ringing the front doorbell?

She made no sound on the plushy turf. The study windows were still open. She had stepped to one of them and raised her hand to tap on a pane, when she was arrested by what she saw within the room.

The fire in the grate was burning brightly now. Someone must have added logs and kindling a moment ago. She could see Cornelius himself in profile standing before the fire. The typescript, still between its blue covers, was in his hands, but he was removing the staples. Now he was tearing the script into strips and feeding them to the flames.

He picked up the Xerox now and did the same thing.

She was too surprised to move or speak. She stood and watched as he unreeled the magnetic tape and tossed it into the fire.

Technicians can sometimes recover a word or two from a tape that has been erased, but they can do nothing with ashes.

Now there was no record at all of anything she had told Cornelius.

Chapter Six

It was one in the morning by the dashboard clock when Marina left the Massachusetts Turnpike for Route 117.

The closer she got to Lincoln, the less she liked the idea of returning to an empty house alone at night.

There was only one other place where she might go uninvited at such an hour, Lettice King's. Did she really know Lettice that well? Perhaps this was a good time to find out.

Lettice was one of the most successful photographers' models of her generation, a Western geisha selling beauty and grace but never brute sex.

She could not be an actress; she was too placid. Tried out once on television, she had walked through her part like a mechanical doll and missed half her cues. But she still had the beauty which her agents called "a valuable property."

She was so regally tall and slim that all clothes looked superb on her, even the grotesque antifashions today that make so many women look like refugees from a prison camp. She had sunshine hair and blue-sky eyes and a delicately classic nose and chin. Nothing could ruffle her serenity. This had attracted Marina to her when they first met during one of the tornadoes that always preceded a deadline at *Home Exquisite*. Laughter and tears were taboo to the geisha of old Japan, because they bring lines to the face prematurely. Lettice needed no such taboo.

Both girls were new to New York, each trying to hide a little loneliness and homesickness. Inevitably they became friends, but the friendship had never been tested as it was going to be tested now.

Coming from the turnpike on Route 117, Lettice's road was about a mile before Marina's. She didn't make up her mind until her headlights picked up Lettice's road sign. Then she found herself taking the turn automatically.

As she shut off her engine, she glanced at the clock again. Nearly two.

She looked up at the house. No lights. Lettice might be away on an assignment in New York or California or even Europe. There was an alternative. Marina could go to a motel alone. The very thought was lonely. She didn't just want a place to sleep. She wanted someone to talk to.

It took a minute or so of pounding on the front door before a window opened upstairs and a sleepy voice called down:

"Who's there?"

"Me. Marina. I'm sorry, but I'm desperate. Please let me in."

"I'll be right down."

Lettice stood in the open doorway, tranquil as if she were posing for a still of what the well-dressed woman will wear at two in the morning. Her dressing gown of heavy, corded silk was a pale, dull pink, severely cut, almost military. Her hair and face were flawless as usual, no puffy lids, no loose tendrils.

She took one look at Marina and drew her into the house.

"You poor child! What's wrong?"

"Everything!" Marina's frail control shattered.

Afterward, her recollection of pouring out her whole story to Lettice was confused, but she had a clear memory of Lettice's steady hand holding a hot drink laced with rum to her lips and Lettice's clear voice saying: "You're going to bed now. We'll talk tomorrow."

On a lower floor there was a guest room with a bed already made. Marina fell into it. The last thing she remembered was Lettice's voice: "You're still shivering. I'm going to switch on the electric blanket . . ."

Sunshine woke her. A clock in a bedside table read five minutes to noon, but the sun had only just reached these western windows.

They were not really windows. They were floor-to-ceiling panels of glass, sliding along grooves. They looked out upon a meadow that sloped down to a lake with woods beyond. Boston seemed hundreds of miles away.

The bedroom was austere, but the builders had let themselves go in the bathroom: a tub like a small swimming pool, a separate shower enclosed in glass, floor tiles and towel rails warmed from inside. How wise of Lettice to rent a house! She could hardly afford to buy one as comfortable as this.

Marina took a hot bath and a cold shower, but she could not feel really fresh when she had to put on once more the crumpled clothes she had lived in for the last twenty-four hours. After airing the bed and spreading the towels to dry, she went upstairs.

"Lettice?"

No answer.

She walked through an archway into the living room.

66

Sunlight poured through another row of sliding glass panels. These led to an outdoor deck. Since her last visit here a wrought-iron stairway had been added to the deck leading down to the meadow. In place of balusters, a procession of little naked men, cast in bronze, supported a railing on their heads, one to each step and each one different. They looked as if they had been frozen in the very act of descending the stairs single file. They had to be the work of Giacometti. No other sculptor could have made them look so hungry and pathetic. But what were they doing here? Did they belong to Lettice or her landlord?

Another archway brought Marina into a compact kitchen at the front of the house near the driveway. Here she found a note propped against the telephone:

Help yourself to breakfast. I'll be back soon.

She found a pitcher of orange juice in the refrigerator and a drip coffeepot on a shelf. She put frozen croissants in the oven and, when everything was ready, she took a tray out to the deck in the sunshine. She was just finishing breakfast when she heard a key in the front door.

Lettice came in carrying groceries. Her blue shirt matched her eyes. Her white shorts revealed her wasp waist and long, tapered legs. A figure like that could sell any fashion, however ugly, to women who believed they would look like Lettice if they wore what she wore.

"Sorry I had to go out," she said.

"Don't be. I found everything. Coffee?"

"Thanks." Lettice brought a cup and saucer for herself out onto the deck. She handed Marina a bundle of letters. "Your mail including yesterday's."

"That looks like a week's accumulation."

"It's only a few days. Victor asked me to collect everything while he was away. I usually pick it up on my way home from work."

"So that's why there was no mail in our box when I looked yesterday afternoon." Marina tossed the junk mail into a scrapbasket and looked at the other letters. They were mostly from neighbors or people working in Victor's office who had read about the accident in the *Boston Globe* or *The New York Times*. Was there anything they could do to help? Neither Cornelius nor Anna had written.

Marina pushed the letters aside. "Do you remember the day when Victor left?"

"Not exactly. About two days after your accident, I think. From the way he talked then, I thought he'd be back in a day or so. Haven't you heard anything from him since he left?"

"Not a word. I'm worried."

Lettice poured herself another cup of coffee. "What are you going to do?"

"There are only two things I can do, go to the police or keep quiet."

"Keeping quiet won't find Victor, will it?"

"Suppose he doesn't want to be found?"

"What makes you think that?"

"Didn't I tell you what dear Cousin Anna said?"

"All that stuff about another woman? Don't you know spite when you hear it?"

"What do you think I should do?"

"Find a lawyer you can trust and let him find Victor for you."

"Lawyers aren't cheap. I have no idea how much money we have in the bank."

" 'We?' "

"Victor and I had—have—a joint checking account."

"Then you can draw anything you need."

"Not until I know exactly how much is there."

"Do you mean you don't know the balance?" Astonishment broke the surface of Lettice's usual blandness.

"I left all that to Victor."

"How wifely!"

"I don't like balancing checkbooks. I was delighted when I found Victor wanted to do it, but now I'll have to call the bank and find out just how much is there."

"They won't tell you on the telephone unless you can identify yourself by telling them the amount of the last deposit."

"I made a small deposit just before the accident. Let's hope that was the last one."

Marina carried her tray back into the kitchen. Lettice, like a well-schooled secretary, looked up the number and dialed it for her.

"I want to check the balance in a joint account . . . Victor and Marina Skinner. . . . The number is 275–636–6 and the last deposit I made was three hundred dollars and no cents. . . . Thank you."

Marina put the telephone back in its cradle slowly.

"Well?"

"There's something wrong."

"No money in the account?"

"Just the opposite. We never kept more than a thousand in that account."

"And now?"

"There's fifty thousand."

Lettice whistled. "In a checking account?"

"Yes. It's not even one of those Now Accounts that do

69

bear a little interest."

"It must be a temporary deposit."

"But where did it come from?"

"A transfer from a savings account?"

"We've never had more than thirty thousand in our savings account."

"A bonus from Cousin Cornelius?"

"How could Victor earn a bonus as large as that? Cousin Cornelius is generous with advice, but not with money."

Lettice lit a cigarette and looked at Marina through the first drift of smoke. "What did Victor actually do at Luka?"

"You're falling into the past tense, too."

"Sorry. What does he do?"

"You'll say I'm being wifely again, but the truth is I don't know much about it. Victor is an administrator and the department he administers is the research department."

"What kind of research?"

"Applied physics. I don't know the details."

"Did Victor try to hide the details from you?"

"He didn't have to." Marina laughed. "He used to bring home notebooks full of equations, but they might as well have been Sanskrit as far as I was concerned. The only things he brought home that interested me were the ciphers."

"Military ciphers?"

"No, multinationals use their own ciphers. They have so many trade secrets they have to."

"And Victor told you all about these ciphers?"

"Don't you believe me?" Marina ran fingers through her tangled locks and looked a little enviously at Lettice's shining hair, sleek and close to her head as a silken cap.

"Oh, I believe you," said Lettice. "There are men like that. I just hadn't realized Victor was one of them."

"He trusted me."

"Obviously, or he would never have left that fifty thousand in a joint account where you were bound to see it. You know it's lucky for you he did. Now you have enough money for lawyers and anything else you need."

"But, Lettice, I can't regard this money as mine."

"Why not?"

"Victor must have needed it for something. He would never have put it in the checking account unless he wanted to draw on it in a day or so."

"Has it occurred to you that someone else may have put it in Victor's account?"

"Why would anyone do that?"

"I can think of various reasons. Do you have enough cash in a savings account to cover lawyers' fees?"

"Probably, but . . . are you sure I need a lawyer? Why don't I just go to the police by myself?"

"What are you going to tell them?"

"The important things: that Victor has disappeared and that I don't know the details because I was in the Sanders Clinic when it happened."

"Aren't you going to tell them that Dr. Sanders kept you in the clinic against your will? And that you were only able to leave the clinic because a stranger convinced Dr. Sanders that he was Victor? And that Victor's Cousin Cornelius is doing nothing about Victor's disappearance except burning your account of what happened?"

"Do you think I ought to bring charges against Dr. Sanders before I can prove them?"

"I think you need a lawyer who will take charge of the whole mess."

"All right, Lettice, but that can wait. What cannot wait a

71

moment longer is telling the police that Victor has disappeared. Where do I go? State, county or town police?"

"I think you want the district attorney," said Lettice. "He has state police officers on his staff assigned to Middlesex County."

"Not Suffolk?"

"Boston is Suffolk. Lincoln is Central Middlesex."

"Would these be the same officers who investigated the accident?"

"Probably. Isn't that all to the good? They know something about your case already. You're bringing them new evidence."

"I'm not sure I like that idea."

"Why not?"

"Dr. Sanders must have talked to them already when they were investigating the accident. They'll see me the way he sees me, a sick woman subject to delusions. Why can't I go to the town police?"

"I doubt if they're equipped for anything more complicated than misdemeanors and minor traffic violations."

"Is there no other place I can go?"

"I suppose you might try the District Court of Lincoln. It's actually in Concord at 305 Walden Street. I had to go there once when vandals were polluting my lake."

"What will happen if I go to them?"

"If you can convince the judge you have a case, he'll turn it over to the grand jury. They have a staff of investigators who collect evidence for indictments, but aren't you being a little paranoid in not trusting the state police?"

"I'm less trusting than I used to be."

"Has Dr. Sanders done that to you?"

"And Cousin Cornelius. Why did he have me make that

72

tape in the first place if he was just going to burn it? What would he have done if I'd remembered to ask for my Xerox copy of my statement before I left?"

"He would have told you that his Xerox machine had broken down and that he only had the one copy he needed himself. Something like that. Don't you recognize his strategy? It's the old ploy of the powerful: never refuse when you can confuse. Distraction and delay are always better than obstruction. In the long run evasion has the same effect as a prompt negative, but evasion does a lot more to wear down morale."

"Why are you smiling?"

"I just thought of something funny. You were asking for trouble by going back to Cornelius unannounced after you had said good-bye. A friend of mine says that no husband who wants to preserve his marriage ever goes home unannounced."

"Your friend is cynical."

"My friend is realistic. You should always avoid putting anybody in a position that may embarrass both of you."

"Is that the new morality?"

"That's manners—always a lot more practical than morals. Now tell me something I've just begun to wonder about. Did that impostor look enough like Victor to fool a bank?"

"I doubt if he could have passed for Victor at Victor's own bank here in Boston, but he might have got away with it at some bank where Victor wasn't known, if he had any of Victor's credit cards for identification, or if he were introduced by someone like Cousin Cornelius. After all, those photographs on some of the credit cards are not good likenesses."

"We always come back to Cousin Cornelius, don't we?"

"I can't help it," said Marina. "Why did he talk about going to the governor himself when he didn't mean a word of it? Just so I would leave everything to him and do nothing myself? Doesn't he want to know what has happened to Victor?"

"Or does he know already?"

"Oh . . ." Marina could not find words to answer this. The possibilities were too horrible.

"The sooner you go to Lincoln District Court the better," said Lettice briskly. "I'd go with you only I have a modeling date in New York this afternoon and I can't break it. I need the money."

"I don't mind going alone, but I'd like to come back here tonight, if I may."

"I was going to suggest that, but there's just one thing: I may not be back until late tonight. Why don't I give you a key so you can make yourself at home until I get back?"

"How thoughtful of you."

"Oh, I'm generous with keys. I gave Victor one when you were in the clinic, so he could use my telephone. He had a funny idea that the telephone at your house was bugged."

Outdoors the sun was warm and a high wind kept the treetops in motion. A dancing day like this could lift the heaviest heart for a few moments.

Besides, Marina was doing something now. Despair comes only when there is nothing you can do.

As she watched for road signs that read Lexington and Concord, she recalled that she was driving through old battlefields. This banal landscape of paved roads, suburban houses and busy shopping centers had once been the scene of war. How different the reality must have been from the

74

cheerful, bloodless, textbook battles children were taught in school. Families divided by conflicting loyalties, wounded and dying without anesthetics or antibiotics . . . the good, old days . . .

The courthouse was only a stone's throw from Walden Pond, but the architect, Robert Charles, had thrown away tradition. The building was all brick. Six tall, narrow arches, guarding a shallow porch, looked Moorish in the oblique light and long shadows of late afternoon. Since she knew it housed The Law, she parked extra close to the curb in a meticulously straight line before she shut off the engine.

Only then did she discover how hard it was going to be to make herself get out of the car and walk into that building.

She sat in the sun, listening to two flags, State and Nation, snapping crisply against their poles in the stiff breeze.

What was the matter with her?

Had it something to do with the blurred figure she could just see through the sheet of glass that formed the front door?

Even when he came through an archway and ran lightly down the steps, she didn't recognize him. It was only when he reached the driveway that his remarkable height began to look familiar. It was only when he passed within a few feet of her without seeing her that she recognized his volcanic profile. In just such random bays and promontories did the edge of molten lava flow and turn to stone.

It was Dr. Sanders.

Chapter Seven

Flight was compulsive. It took the form of aimless driving around back roads to give herself time to think.

She had realized that officers of the district court would talk to Dr. Sanders after she told them her story, but she had not foreseen that Dr. Sanders might get a story of his own in first.

What had he told them? That she was a patient he had been tricked into releasing prematurely, a potential danger to herself and to others?

Had he talked to other law enforcement officers? If he had talked only to those at the district court, why had he chosen them?

It seemed only too likely that any such officers would listen more sympathetically to his story than to hers. He had the prestige of the Sanders Clinic and his own reputation behind him. He had an authoritative manner and a professional vocabulary that would impress laymen. He would surely have the support of his fellow psychiatrists, closing ranks against the psychologically illiterate.

No doubt there would be consultations and second opinions, but who would take her word against his? Eventually she would be sent back to his clinic "for observation," and now that she had demonstrated so dramatically her will to escape, Dr. Sanders would see to it that she did not have the chance to do so again.

For some time a traitor idea had been lurking at the back of her mind which she had not dared to face before even in the privacy of her own thoughts. Now this enemy thought moved into the foreground of her thinking.

Suppose . . . just suppose . . . Dr. Sanders was right?

Suppose there was something wrong with her? Would she be able to recognize such a flaw in herself? Wasn't there a theory that no people are more vehemently certain of their sanity than the insane?

The story she had told Cornelius and Lettice could so easily be construed as paranoid fantasy. Was she seeing threats where there were none? Plots and stratagems where there was only good will? Was that why Cornelius had destroyed the tape as soon as he heard her story? Was that why Lettice had urged her to seek help from the law immediately?

There was a long list of debatable things she would have to prove in order to substantiate her story.

That the accident was caused by another car, driven by an an unknown man.

That she was pregnant at the time.

That she had not been drinking at the time.

That Dr. Sanders had kept her in the clinic against her will.

That he had tried to make her believe that her story of the accident was false.

That Victor had disappeared while she was in the clinic.

That a stranger had come to the clinic pretending to be

Victor and had then disappeared himself.

That without her knowledge Victor, or someone else, had deposited an inexplicably large sum in the checking account she shared with Victor.

Of all these things, only one was supported by tangible evidence. There was an unexplained deposit in the checking account.

Everything else depended on her memory alone unless she could get corroboration from Victor himself. . . .

Something familiar about the road brought her attention back to reality. Surely she knew those two lilac bushes leaning over that dry-stone wall and the mailbox that sat crookedly on its post at the foot of this driveway.

Something clicked like the sudden discovery of hidden faces in a puzzle picture. She was looking at her own driveway. Her reflexes had brought her here like a homing pigeon.

In her grandmother's day an old horse would sometimes find his way back to a house where he had lived years ago while his driver was thinking of something else. People used to say the horse "knew" the way. Wasn't it more likely that the driver had guided the horse unconsciously just as she had guided her car just now? What had brought her back? Was she trying to return to past happiness?

Yesterday, in a dim light, the house had looked deserted. Today it was transfigured in a bath of golden light from the late sun, a bright vision of everybody's dream house where nothing could ever go wrong.

The little red flag on the mailbox was up. Mail delivered since Lettice's last collection? Of course. She had not said that she had picked up this morning's delivery.

Marina pulled over to the side of the road and emptied the box. There were a dozen envelopes. One caught her eye, a long brown envelope, the kind the bank used for statements.

Everything about the statement itself was normal and correct except for that one thing—the inexplicable deposit of fifty thousand dollars, added to the balance just about the time Victor went to Iran.

A computer mistake?

As she stood looking at the figures she heard the faint ringing of a bell in the distance. It came and went rhythmically like the ringing of a telephone. . . .

It was a telephone. It was faint only because it was ringing inside the house.

She stuffed the other letters into her handbag and ran up the driveway. She clawed the key out of her handbag and wrenched the door open. The ringing was loud as she tore down the hall. Each time it paused she caught her breath for fear it would not ring again.

She stumbled as she plunged into the cubbyhole under the stairs and snatched the telephone from its cradle, still ringing.

"Victor?"

Now there was nothing but a dial tone.

She dropped into a chair to catch her breath. If only she had run a little faster . . .

As her breathing came back to normal, she decided to go upstairs and look among the papers in the desk there to see if anything suggested a normal provenance for that fifty thousand dollars.

Halfway up the stairs, she looked down, through an archway, into the living room. Again she saw the glass on the table near Victor's chair. It was half filled with a dark liquid. Whiskey? But hadn't it been empty yesterday? She couldn't remember.

The large bedroom at the back of the house, overlooking the garden, was the one she and Victor had shared. There were windows in three walls of that room and nothing beyond them but fields, trees and sky. On clear nights they could lie in each other's arms and still see the stars.

She crossed the room to the desk that stood between two of the windows and lowered the drop leaf.

She started with the pigeonholes. The first things she found were two passports, hers and Victor's. Didn't you need a passport to go to Iran?

Other pigeonholes were filled with bills to pay and letters to answer. Nothing that could not be left there a little longer.

At last a shallow drawer yielded the things she was looking for, the savings bank passbook and the recent deposit slips for the checking account. There was no withdrawal of fifty thousand dollars recorded in the savings passbook, and there was no deposit slip for fifty thousand dollars in the checking account. She put the passbook and the deposit slips in her handbag. These things were evidence that Victor might need to clear himself someday.

She closed the desk flap so she could get at the larger drawers underneath it. She found nothing there that was important to her at this moment. Just old income tax records and old real estate tax receipts.

Every now and then she found herself stopping to listen to the silence.

Were all empty houses haunted?

Better get out of here before she started imagining things.

She took one last look around the room and stepped into the hall. For a moment she hesitated before the closed door opposite, then threw it open.

No crib, no small sheets and blankets, but that might be

explained. Victor might have thought it would be easier for her not to see them when she came home from the clinic.

She shut the door and turned toward the stairs.

What would she be like if she had never met Victor? Would she have gone on alone after *Home Exquisite* folded, content with another job on some other magazine and a series of loveless affairs until she was too old for either love or work and there was nothing left but a small pension and a lonely country cottage?

Only a year ago such a future would have seemed sufficient if not desirable, but not now. Birds who have known flight cannot be happy with clipped wings.

So what would she do if Victor never came back? Live alone in this house with all its memories? Oh, no, she would have to sell the house.

Strangers would come to live here who knew Victor and herself only through hearsay. Who planted those roses? The Skinners who lived here before. Who put that awful wallpaper in the guest room? The Skinners. What were they like? No one remembers them. They were only here a short while.

It will be a haunted house for those strangers, and it is we who will be the ghosts, Victor and I. When they hear a sound like a footfall in an empty room or see a shadow where there is no substance, they will laugh and say: "It must be the Skinners!"

And who knows? Maybe it will be. How absurd to assume that ghosts know when they are haunting a house. Much more likely haunting is involuntary, unremembered and unreal to ghosts themselves as dreams are to the living. Perhaps it is a more frightening experience to be the haunter instead of the haunted. . . .

On the stairs the windows were red with the last rays of

the sun. She hurried into the kitchen to make sure the back door was locked. She was turning back towards the dining room when she heard someone at the front door.

No one knew she was here, not even Lettice. She had not opened windows or turned on lights or—

Wait a minute. She had left her car at the foot of the driveway when she ran into the house to answer the telephone and then forgotten all about it. Anyone who recognized her car would know she was here.

The front door locked automatically when it was shut and it was shut now. Perhaps whoever was there would go away when he found he couldn't get in.

She stood still, listening.

Was that a key in the lock?

If she tried to leave the kitchen by going through the dining room into the hall, she would be running directly into the arms of anyone at the front door, but she might still escape by going through the kitchen and dining room to the living room where there was a door to the garden.

She was halfway across the kitchen when she heard the front door open. She had almost reached the door to the dining room when a man's voice spoke:

"Stop!"

She turned her head.

He was standing on the threshold of the door that led from the hall into the kitchen, in such deep shadow she could barely see his face He was just a tall man with dark hair.

At that moment she had no idea whether this was the impostor or Victor himself.

Chapter Eight

"What are you doing here?"

"I saw your car in the driveway. Naturally I wanted to speak to my wife." He moved forward out of the shadows and she saw that he was smiling.

"Let's stop playing games," she said. "I don't know who you are or what you want, but I do know you are not Victor."

His smile was indestructible. "What makes you so sure?"

"I was sure the moment I kissed you."

He was not pleased, but it barely showed. He had himself well in hand. "Why did you do that?"

"I had to convince Dr. Sanders that I really believed you were my husband, and I had to do it quickly."

"It must have taken nerve."

"It did."

"Was there anything else that gave me away?"

"Everything else gave you away to me. When you care for a man you notice things about him you wouldn't notice otherwise. They say the very pupils of your eyes open wider when you look at someone you care about. It wasn't just your face or your voice or the big things you did. It was the little things."

"Such as?"

"Victor would never have left me alone here without warning yesterday. You did. Why?"

"I wanted to see what you would do."

"There wasn't any noise outside, was there?"

"No."

"Why did you say there was?"

"Perhaps I don't trust you any more than you trust me, but I have done one thing for you. I helped you fool Dr. Sanders."

"Did you?"

"Obviously. Dr. Sanders would never have let you walk out with me if he had not believed I was Victor."

"But what else could he have done after he had introduced you to me as Victor before all those nurses? How do I know that you and Dr. Sanders are not in this together? If I had reacted to the introduction normally and denied that you were Victor, I would have given Dr. Sanders a perfect excuse to keep me in the clinic indefinitely, and I think that is what he was trying to do when he let you come there. The one thing neither you nor he could have anticipated was what I did: acknowledging you publicly as my husband."

"You've got the whole thing all wrong. I never saw Dr. Sanders before yesterday and he had never seen me before. I came there to get you out of the clinic in spite of Dr. Sanders."

"What made you think I would walk out with you when I had no idea who you were?"

"I had cased the joint."

"What do you mean?"

84

"One of the nurses had been fired. I talked to her."

"Amelia Conrad?"

"That's the one. Nice little thing. She was worried about you and didn't know what to do. She thought you were being held in the clinic against your will and would do anything to get out. I told her I'd help you. Before I tackled Dr. Sanders, I tried to find out more about you by looking you up in old microfilms of *The New York Times*. It was there I came across a wedding picture of you and your husband. I saw at once that Victor Skinner and I were about the same height, build and coloring. I checked with various sources in New York and found that apparently Victor Skinner and Eric Sanders had never met. The rest was easy. You jumped at the chance I gave you."

"Suppose I hadn't. Suppose I had said: 'This is not my husband.' "

"I would have fallen back on your unfortunate tendency to amnesia. Dr. Sanders could hardly have disputed that. He had been telling Amelia Conrad and everyone else that your memory was seriously affected by your concussion."

"Why?"

"Why what?"

"Why did you do all this?"

He glanced at the only chairs in the kitchen, hard and uncomfortable as most kitchen chairs.

"Can't we talk someplace else?"

"Let's go into the living room."

As they entered it the half-empty glass of whiskey caught her eye again.

"Yours?"

"No. I may make free with other people's houses, but I don't help myself to their whiskey. That glass might be worth examining for fingerprints. May I?"

"Why not? You'll probably just find old prints of Victor's, and he has more right to be in the house than you have."

He looked at her thoughtfully. "You aren't afraid of me anymore?"

"You're no longer a mystery," she answered. "I know you're not Victor and I believe you when you say you're not working for Dr. Sanders."

"But you still don't know who I am or why I'm here."

"That doesn't make you a mystery. Just a puzzle. I'm sure there's a simple explanation. Tell me. Why did you get me out of the clinic and why are you here now?"

"Which question shall I answer first?"

"Why don't you begin by telling me your name?"

"Quentin Yardley."

"And your job?"

"I'm employed by the CCIE to investigate the leakage of American trade secrets to foreign competitors."

"CCIE?"

"Congressional Committee on Industrial Espionage."

"So all this is just a matter of business?"

"You can't separate industrial and military espionage anymore. Trade secrets are usually military secrets as well. When they are leaked to foreign competitors, they are also leaked to foreign governments."

"But are there really any military secrets left? I thought every nation, big or small, had its own dear, little nuclear bomb now, in the arsenal or on the drawing board."

"Technical refinements are still being developed."

"Do technical refinements matter so much?"

"They are worth a great deal of money."

"What's a great deal? Fifty thousand dollars?"

"Oh, no, a great deal more than that."

"What has this to do with Victor or me?"

"We have reason to believe there has been a leakage of technical information at Luka, Incorporated."

"To a foreign government?"

"To an Iranian company incorporated in France, the Société Anonyme Mazda; in English, Mazda, Limited. Four things happened all about the same time. Mazda acquired a certain industrial secret, your husband disappeared on a trip to Iran, you were involved in an accident that nearly killed you and then detained against your will at the Sanders Clinic. I think these things are all connected."

It was fortunate for Marina that Quentin Yardley could not read her mind. At this moment every other thought was crowded out by one thing, that fifty-thousand-dollar deposit. Surely Victor would never keep a record of the taking of a bribe so openly? Victor was not stupid. There must be some other explanation for that deposit.

"Are you suggesting that Victor was involved in this theft?" she said aloud.

"I'm not accusing anybody yet," said Quentin.

"Why did you come here today?"

"To see if Victor Skinner is still having mail sent here."

Was this man looking for a bank statement? Or did he hope to catch Victor, if Victor came to collect his own mail?

"A neighbor of ours picks up all our mail now," said Marina.

"I know that, but I go through it every afternoon before she gets here, just to see if there's anything interesting."

Marina thought: if I had not picked up the mail, he would have seen that bank statement.

"I know what you're thinking," said Quentin.

"Do you?" It was all she could do to keep her voice level.

"You're thinking this seems like an invasion of privacy."

"It is an invasion of privacy," said Marina. "And undoubtedly illegal."

"When you work for the CCIE, you have to cut corners sometimes, but you ought to trust me because I'm the only person who can help you find your husband. No one else is looking for him."

"Aren't people at Luka looking for him?"

"My information is that they aren't looking very hard. Their chief concern is keeping this business out of the newspapers. They're probably afraid Victor Skinner has gone over to Mazda. They wouldn't want a thing like that in the papers. It might harm them as much as Mazda."

"But there's nothing to connect Victor with Mazda?"

"Not yet, but he did disappear on a trip to Iran, and Mazda is an Iranian company."

"Have you thought of investigating Mazda?"

"Other men are doing that. My beat is at this end, and I've already found one thing in Skinner's mail that may be significant."

"What?"

His eyes narrowed with calculation. Perhaps it was to justify the pause that he offered her a cigarette. When she shook her head impatiently, he lit one for himself and inhaled deeply.

"Mrs. Skinner, if I am going to trust you any farther, I must have your word that you will not tell anyone else the things I tell you."

"There isn't anyone I'd be likely to tell except Victor, and he isn't here."

"What about this friend you're staying with, Miss King, isn't it?"

"Lettice is a fashion model. She's not interested in military or industrial secrets."

Perhaps it was a quibble, but she had managed not to give him a promise that she wouldn't talk in so many words. Had he realized that?

Apparently not, for now, without another word, he took an envelope out of his breast pocket and handed it to her.

"This was in the mailbox three days after your accident. Notice anything about it?"

"It's one of the small, stamped envelopes you can buy at any post office."

"Look at the address."

"It was sent to Victor here. There's no return address."

"And the handwriting?"

"Why . . . it's Victor's own writing!"

"Exactly. If a man is carrying a document that he fears may be stolen from him at any moment, what does he usually do?"

"Oh . . . he mails it to himself, but, in that case, Victor must have expected to be here when the letter arrived."

"Not necessarily. He may have assumed that you or Miss King would be here and save the letter for him without opening it."

"But you opened it." She had trouble keeping anger out of her voice as she looked down and saw the torn flap of the envelope.

"Better look inside," said Quentin. "If you want to help your husband you mustn't be squeamish about going through his mail."

Marina took out a single sheet of paper, folded once. "It's in cipher."

"Does that surprise you?"

"Not really. Multinationals use cipher all the time."

"Can you read this one?"

There was no point in letting the enemy know that cipher breaking was one of Victor's hobbies and that he had taught her a good bit about it.

She made her face expressionless as she looked down at the ciphertext, nineteen lines of letters in groups of five, ending with:

RGAAN OYQLS EILZK KGNYS OQZPD ER
IUFMB MPYCC HDODP KCIUS CCSJT EIB
RFBIJ EMVOR NJHWQ QDZDI ACOW
EZHVL XKSAQ ITKRV XQZGY DZA

Why had he ended each line with a group of letters less than five? Why hadn't he added nulls, meaningless cipher symbols used to make each group of letters the same length and so confuse anyone trying to break the cipher?

Now she had to lie, she tried to make it sound as convincing as possible.

"What do you take me for? I could never read a ciphertext without the key word."

Quentin put out his cigarette and rose.

"You're forgetting that glass." She spoke quickly, hoping to distract him from the ciphertext still in her hand.

"Glass?"

"The tumbler of whiskey. Weren't you going to take it with you and have it examined for fingerprints?"

"Oh, yes. Have you something I can put it in?"

"There's probably a paper bag in the kitchen."

He moved toward the dining room. The moment his back was turned, she slid the ciphertext into her handbag, keeping the empty envelope in one hand.

I am becoming as devious as he is. The thought dismayed her but not enough to shake her resolution.

In the kitchen she found him a small carton.

"Wouldn't this be better than a bag?"

"Much better. Thanks."

She handed him the empty envelope and held her breath until he put it back in his breast pocket without looking inside. Perhaps he would not discover that the envelope was empty until he got back to his office, wherever that was.

"Better not stay here alone tonight," he said. "Whoever drank that whiskey might come back."

"I'll be all right. I'm staying at Lettice King's again tonight."

As soon as he had gone, Marina took pencil and paper from the memo pad beside the telephone and began to work on the cipher.

It was practically impossible to break a cipher with mathematical analysis alone when you had only one ciphertext of only nineteen lines to work with, but if you could combine mathematical with psychological analysis, you had a slim chance.

And what was the basis of psychological analysis? Knowing the context of the message, the circumstances, mind and verbal habits of the man who had enciphered it, in this case Victor, whom Marina knew so well.

He had scrawled the address on the envelope in furious

haste. Assume he had enciphered the message in the same haste. What was the quickest cipher he would be likely to use?

She knew the answer. Victor liked variations on the old Vigenère tableau, and it did work quickly if you set it up on a Saint Cyr slide rule, earliest forerunner of modern cipher machines.

With pen, paper and scissors you could make the slide rule in two minutes and burn the evidence after you were through.

Victor had memorized two incoherent alphabets, the letters in order of their frequency in English text and the letters in order of the typewriter keyboard. They were easy for him to remember because he had occasion to use both of them so often. In a hurry he would use one on the slide and one on the index. He liked running keys, preferably incoherent, so the key word might be anything. She would guess at the cleartext and let the key develop itself from the relation between the hypothetical cleartext and the actual ciphertext.

She lost all track of time. She was scarcely conscious of twilight seeping into the room like a slowly rising tide of shadow until she felt the need for more light.

When she switched on the lamp its sudden radiance seemed to illuminate mind as well as eyes. Now she could see clearly that one small corner in the third line of the ciphertext was beginning to crumble. Was she on the verge of penetrating the cipher?

Thirty minutes later she looked at the text she had teased out of the tangle and knew she was right so far. She had got the whole third line and the words were so familiar that she could fill in all the other lines from memory without doing any more work on the cipher.

It was an old French song, a children's song, part of a game. Victor's father had brought the book home from a trip to France. Victor's mother had made this translation for him when he was a small boy fascinated by pictures in the book. She admitted it was a free translation. It had to be in order to fit English syllables to the tempo of the French air. She thought it didn't matter because there were different versions of the song in French.

It was the twelfth stanza which fixed Marina's attention now.

> *Come whenever midnight strikes,*
> *Companions of the Sweet Marjoram . . .*
> *Midnight has already struck,*
> *Blithe, blithe, over the pier . . .*

How odd it was that words repeated in cleartext, like midnight and blithe, never showed up as repeated letter groups in ciphertext. That was the glory of intricate cipher systems like this double substitution. No letter was ever enciphered the same way twice.

But what could the song mean to Victor now? Why had he gone to all the trouble of putting it into cipher and mailing it to himself?

Marina searched her memory for everything he had ever said about it.

"Scared the living daylights out of me when I was eight." He had said that when they first came across the song unpacking family books which he had put in storage after his parents' death.

"But why? It's not a scary song."

"It was to me. Always. Maybe because the picture shows

the man in the moon with such a look of horror on his face. Or maybe because the air is in such a haunting minor key. Don't you feel anything menacing about it?"

"Not particularly, but then I'm not eight years old. Who were the Companions of the Sweet Marjoram?"

"I haven't the slightest idea, but I always felt there was nothing sweet about them. The whole thing is really more like a rather sinister little stage play than a child's game, a conflict between a stray Captain of the Watch and a timid father of marriageable daughters, all in dialogue.

"The opening line sets the mood: *Who comes by this way so late?* Perfect beginning for a murder mystery. Everything about the scene is enigmatic. Why does the refrain cry, 'Blithe, blithe,' when the song itself is saturated with quiet menace? Why is the Captain so bold in pressing his suit and the father so evasive in putting him off? Why do the father and daughters live on or near a pier? And where is the mother?"

"You thought of all this as a child?"

"Children have more imagination than people realize. I never could escape a shiver when we came to that climactic line: *Midnight has already struck . . .* Why didn't the father know that it was midnight? Or did he know? Was he just trying to make the Captain believe that it was earlier than he thought?"

None of this explained why Victor had suddenly decided to hide that climactic line in a ciphertext. . . .

A new idea came to her.

Could this be encicode? The two-step cryptogram the French call *code chiffré?*

The process is simple. First, you encode a cleartext. Second, you encipher that codetext.

To retrieve the cleartext with nothing to work on but the ciphertext you have to reverse the two-step process. First, you have to break the ciphertext to get the codetext. Second, you have to break the codetext to get the cleartext.

No, that wouldn't work.

This French song was a coherent text. By its very nature a codetext must be as incoherent as a ciphertext.

She saw just one possible exception, the paradox called "open code," the trickiest code of all.

According to David Kahn, brilliant historian of cryptography, an open code consists of ordinary words which two groups of people have agreed to invest with symbolic meaning.

An open codetext by its very nature has to be a coherent text so it can pass for normal communication. Like the microdot it tries to hide the very fact of its existence. Unlike the microdot, it can rarely be detected. Symbolism is too subtle for analysis.

The most famous open code message in history may be the one the Japanese Government sent to its air force before Pearl Harbor: HIGASHI NO KAZE AME . . . EAST WIND RAIN.

It escaped detection, but anyone familiar with Japanese thought and idiom could have guessed that EAST WIND RAIN meant WAR WITH AMERICA. In Japan, America is the East, and, the world over, wind and rain mean stormy weather.

And so what about *Midnight has already struck?*

Were those words open code now?

She sat staring at the puzzle until she could almost hear Victor's voice paraphrasing David Kahn:

"No one ever broke a cipher by sitting and staring at it. Do something!"

But she couldn't think of anything to do.

95

At last she told herself that it had been a good try, but no more. She was fighting tears as she refolded the paper. It was then that her eye caught a few words penciled on the wrong side:

1254-A Beacon Street, Apt. 4.

The handwriting was not Victor's. Was it Quentin Yardley's?

The address was at the Brookline end of Beacon Street, a neighborhood she didn't know.

Perhaps she ought to find out more about it before she ventured there alone after dark.

She tried Lettice's number.

No answer.

Then she remembered. Lettice should be in New York by this time.

Whom else could she call?

Only one other person knew where she was now. Why not make use of him? What harm could it do?

If the handwriting was his, it meant he knew this place in Brookline. Wouldn't apparent openness on her part be disarming? Wouldn't it make him think she had accepted him as an ally?

Suppose he had discovered the loss of the ciphertext by this time and demanded its return? Well, she would just return it. She had a copy of it now, and she doubted if he would be able to break it when she, who knew Victor so well, had failed.

The Boston telephone book did not list a regional office for the Congressional Committee on Industrial Espionage, but Directory Assistance in Washington gave her a number for the national headquarters without any trouble.

The soft, southern voice was so friendly that she asked if

the office was likely to be open after five o'clock?

"Yes, ma'am. We get calls for that number up to ten or eleven o'clock at night. They're working long hours over there right now."

Marina dialed the number and got a busy signal. After two more tries another southern voice came on the line.

"CCIE, Walter Tomkins speaking."

"I'm calling from Massachusetts. Do you have a telephone number where I can reach one of your investigating staff here, Mr. Quentin Yardley?"

"Mr. Quentin who?"

"Yardley."

"Just a minute, please, ma'am."

The line hummed. Beyond the humming she could hear voices, but the words were indistinct.

Then the southern voice came back on the line.

"I'm real sorry, ma'am, but seems like you've made some sort of mistake. There's nobody named Quentin Yardley here or in Massachusetts working for the Committee on Industrial Espionage. What's more, there never has been."

Chapter Nine

Marina had not realized that Beacon Street was so long. A sea mist, rolling in from the harbor, made driving difficult. Each street lamp wore a halo of light, frail and silvery as a dandelion gone to seed, so dim that it did more to confuse than clarify the area around it. Tonight the windshield was clouding on the inside, so wipers were not much use.

She slowed to a snail's pace and tried to hug the curb, but she couldn't because a solid row of parked cars was in her way. Every now and then she had to detour around an extra car that was double parked. This took her into the middle of the road where there was always danger of meeting another car coming the other way. That was a real hazard tonight because the fog made it impossible for her to see any other car until it was almost upon her.

If this kept up, Lettice's return plane from New York might not be able to land at Logan tonight.

In Kenmore Square, a huge triangle of scarlet light winked on and off like a monstrous eye drawing attention to the brand name of a motor fuel. How whimsical it was to use up fuel generating electricity for a sign urging motorists to use still more fuel when at any moment there might be another fuel shortage.

Now the stately old brownstones of the Back Bay were giving way to tacky new buildings with shops on the ground floor and offices or dwellings on the floors above.

She passed a huge motel and then, as if some wizard had waved a wand, Beacon Street changed once more. Now there were churches and synagogues and new apartment houses set back from the road among their own lawns. Some suburban frame houses had survived the bulldozer, and there were even a few Victorian mansions still standing among old shade trees and neglected gardens. Some bore signs that read FOR SALE, other signs announced APARTMENTS TO LET, but all were set so far back from the curb that Marina could not read their street numbers.

At last she came to an empty parking place. She pulled into it quickly and walked up a flagstone path to the veranda of the nearest house. Her flashlight beam picked out molded brass figures on the front door: 1240. She had still to pass seven houses before she came to 1254–A.

She drove on slowly, counting the houses as she went by. All parking places in front of the eighth house were taken, but it was near a corner, so she found a place to park in the side street, turned off the ignition, and got out of the car.

Number 1254–A was High Victorian, standing in an acre of its own grounds. It was surrounded by a tall, thick hedge that looked as if it had taken a hundred years to grow. A gravel driveway led through iron gates to a porte cochère. The gates were closed, but there was a smaller gap in the hedge guarded only by a little wooden gate. It opened at a touch upon a footpath which led to the front door.

As Marina walked up the path she was assailed by an

uncanny feeling that she was taking an irrevocable step which she might regret.

What did she know about this place? Nothing, except that Quentin Yardley had thought it necessary to pencil the address on the back of a message in code which he had stolen from Victor.

What was she going to find here now? Could there be anything here that Victor himself might not wish her to discover?

She thought of Pandora and Bluebeard's wife and all the other legendary figures who had not known when to leave well enough alone, but she walked on, past the porte cochère, and looked up at the house.

A hall light shone through two opaque glass panels in the front door. One other light burned in a stained glass window on the floor above.

She went up three shallow steps to an open, communal vestibule. There were four bells and slots for name cards. One slot was empty. The others displayed names that meant nothing to her: Crashaw, Levinson, Diego.

She was about to ring one of the bells at random when she saw that the door was standing ajar. She stepped inside, closing the door behind her.

A large hall with a high ceiling. A parquet floor where once there must have been what they had called Turkey carpets. Now there were only sisal mats. There was still a handsome staircase with the generous proportions that Chippendale gave to his chairs. It looked like solid wood—oak, chestnut or even mahogany. It was hard to tell in the dim light from the Tiffany shaded lamp on the newel-post.

The hall might look shabby by daylight, but in this lamplight it was all nostalgia. Marina could almost see Victorian children playing doll's house on the square landing and a Henry James lady coming down the steps in leg o' mutton sleeves and a tulip skirt.

As the only other light she had seen came from the floor above, Marina started up the stairs.

The hall above was in darkness, but a hairline of light edged the closed door of a room at the front of the house.

Before she could knock, the door was swept open.

"What are you doing here?"

Marina was face to face with Anna Skinner.

She would not have been surprised if Anna had shut the door in her face, but Anna didn't.

She opened it wider and spoke imperiously. "Come in!"

The room ran the whole width of the house. There was a window seat in front of a wide bay window of Victorian stained glass, the dull descendant of the jeweled glass of the Middle Ages. This was the upstairs window where Marina had seen a light when she first approached the house.

The furniture was as worn and scuffed as all furniture let to transients. Refinished, some of it might have passed for "Victorian antique." In this condition it was merely second-hand.

Anna sat in a rocking chair. "How did you get this address?"

"I found it among my husband's papers."

"How did you get in?"

"The door was ajar."

"I didn't leave it that way."

"Then someone else—"

But Anna cut her short. "Nonsense! There's no one else here. Sit down."

Marina sat on the windowseat and put her handbag down

101

on the cushion beside her.

"So Victor knows . . ." Anna's voice sank to a whisper.

"Knows what?" demanded Marina.

"That my son, Thereon, is living here. His own father doesn't know. I thought nobody knew. Even I had the devil of a time finding him here."

"Why is he hiding?"

"I don't know, and the poor boy won't tell me."

"Then you aren't really angry with your son?"

"No, but I want Cornelius to think I am. Then he won't suspect that I am communicating with the boy. If he discovered that, he'd have me followed so he could find out where Thereon is."

"Then Thereon is hiding from his father?"

"There's more to it than that. Cornelius wants to find Thereon, but not for love. He is the one who is angry at Thereon, not me."

"Because Thereon dropped out of Harvard?"

"Cornelius didn't like that, but this is different. It must be something that happened after Thereon dropped out. He's afraid of his father now. He goes nowhere and he sees no one but me. He only sees me because I've promised him secrecy. That's why I can't understand his confiding in Victor. They were never close friends, but Thereon must have given Victor this address. Why?"

"They are cousins."

"As if kinship mattered today!"

Anna lit a cigarette with hands that shook. A palsy is hard to fake. This was not acting. Anna was afraid of something herself. Was that the cause of her constant irritability? Wasn't anger the active form of fear?

"Where is Thereon tonight?"

"I have no idea. He knew I was coming. He gave me a key so I could get in when he wasn't here and wait for him. I've been waiting now for over an hour."

"Is the house often empty?"

"The Crashaws and Levinsons are usually away on weekends. That's why I try to come here on Saturday or Sunday, so no one will see me."

"And the Diegos?"

"Diego is the name Thereon uses here."

"But why do you have to hide from Thereon's neighbors?"

"My picture gets in the papers now and then. There's a remote chance that one of them might identify Thereon through me. He doesn't want to take that chance if he can help it."

"But why?"

"He won't tell me." Anna closed her eyes. She seemed to be fighting tears.

"What does Thereon do with himself all alone here day after day?"

"He says he's writing a book. He won't tell me what it's about. He says I'll never know because he's going to publish it under a pen name."

The glimmer of an idea came to Marina. "Then maybe he is hiding from people who don't want the book published?"

"I suppose that's possible." Anna opened her eyes and rose. She began to walk about the room as if she could not make herself sit still any longer.

"Could his father be one of the people who want to censor this book?"

"Perhaps."

"How many people know about the book?"

"How can I say? I have no idea who his friends are or his

103

enemies. He grew up at the height of the rebellion against parents. He hates his father. He just tolerates me because he's sorry for me. He doesn't love me."

But you love him, thought Marina.

Aloud she said: "Could he feel sorry for you if he had no love for you at all?"

"Of course he could. You feel delightfully superior to other people when you're sorry for them, but you don't love them."

She glanced at the watch on her wrist. "I can't wait any longer. It will take me hours to get back to Greenwich in this fog. If I'm not back by eleven, Cornelius will ask all sorts of questions. He might even begin to suspect that I've been seeing Thereon. I promised the boy I would not let that happen. Are you going to wait for him?"

"A little longer."

"Why do you want to see Thereon?"

"He may know where Victor is. That's the only lead I have."

Anna considered this in silence for a moment.

"I wouldn't stay too long if I were you. It isn't fun being alone at night in a house as large and old and creaky as this, especially when you're listening for someone who never comes. You can imagine all sorts of odd noises."

"Did you?"

"Of course. So don't say I didn't warn you."

"But you stayed. I'll try to hold my imagination in check as you did."

At the door Anna looked back.

"If Thereon comes in later, please ask him to call me no matter how late it is. I'm worried."

Marina listened to the footfalls receding down the uncarpeted stairs, across the lower hall between the sisal mats. She heard the front door close decisively. She thought about its standing ajar when she arrived. Anna would not have left it so. She had a key of her own. She would do nothing to endanger her son.

Had someone else entered the house after Anna, before Marina? Someone who might have left the front door open inadvertently? Was this the explanation of the "odd noises" Anna believed she had imagined?

An uncomfortable thought.

It was one thing to be alone in an empty house and quite another to share an empty house with an unknown, uninvited fellow guest.

At this very moment Marina heard a creak that might have been the response of old timber to the drop in temperature at nightfall and might equally well have been something else.

She was doing exactly what Anna had predicted, imagining things.

To distract her unruly fancy she rose and began to look about the room for some indication that Victor had been there.

Her search didn't take long. Thereon's clothes were few and stylishly grubby: unpressed jeans, soiled shirts, frayed sweaters, scuffed sneakers and a quilted parka for cold weather.

The authors represented on the bookshelves were mostly philosophers. Had Thereon been a philosophy major? The only magazines were old copies of *Nature* and *The Smithsonian,* with the *Bulletin of the Atomic Scientists* at the bottom of the pile.

There were no signs of a literary work in progress. No

typescript, no typewriter. Just a notebook with a few short notes contrasting Spinoza and Whitehead. Who would want to censor a book about Spinoza and Whitehead?

As the minutes ticked by, Marina became depressed with a sense of her own futility. The one hope that might have led her to Victor had led to nothing but a little information about his cousin, Thereon, who meant nothing to her at all.

She was wasting time here. Better get back to Lettice's house and have a good night's rest so she could set out to look for a lawyer the first thing in the morning.

She left the single light burning in Thereon's room and went slowly down the stairs.

At the front door, she paused.

Once again it was ajar.

Surely she had heard it close when Anna left the house?

Could there be something wrong with the lock so it wouldn't stay shut?

Marina set the latch, stepped outside and pulled the door shut behind her. The lock made the same decisive snap she had heard when Anna left the house.

She tried the door.

It wouldn't open.

She started down the path, her depression reflected in her listless pace. When she had passed through the little gate in the hedge, she turned around to close it behind her and lifted her eyes to take a last look at the house.

The stained glass window in Thereon's room was open.

A man was looking out. The light from the street lamp at the corner shone directly on his face.

It was Victor.

Chapter Ten

For a moment she was stunned.

Then a cry was torn from her throat.

"Victor . . ."

The face at the window did not turn toward her. It took her another moment to realize that such a faint cry must have been drowned in the traffic noise at this end of Beacon Street.

She was standing under a tree in a pool of shadow between two areas of dim light diffused from the street lamp at the corner and the glass panels in the front door. Contrast made the shadowy place almost as blinding as darkness itself. The chances were that he could not see her at all.

She opened her mouth to cry out more loudly, but just at that moment the head turned and the face vanished from the window.

She ran up the path to the front door. Only a moment ago she had shut it with the latch set to lock it. Now she took off one of her shoes and struck the glass panel with its heel. The heavy glass was not even cracked.

She ran back to the path and found a stone under the

hedge. She threw it and the glass splintered. She maneuvered one wrist through a ring of lethal spikes and released the lock. The door swung wide.

The stained glass window in Thereon's room was still open, but no one was standing there now. She had not met Victor on the stairs. Where would he have gone if he were looking for Thereon?

Wait a minute. Victorian mansions had back stairs.

She opened a door at the far end of the upper hall. She had guessed right. There was a tight spiral of steep steps enclosed between bare walls without windows. She could not see beyond the first curve, but she heard a door close at the bottom.

She hurried down the stairs and snatched the door open. The large, high-ceilinged kitchen was empty.

It had been modernized. Electric stove and refrigerator, dishwasher, clothes washer and drier were all there, but there was also a brick chimney sporting a tin plate over the outlet where an old stovepipe had once served a range burning wood or coal.

There were four other doors besides the door to the back stairs, one to a butler's pantry and a dining room beyond, one to a small room where an icebox must have stood when ice was delivered by hand, one to a laundry room where old tubs were still built in as part of the wall, and beyond the laundry room, was the door to a back porch.

That door was standing open.

Marina raced along a path that went through a kitchen garden and around thehouse.

No one in sight.

She stood still in the bitterness of defeat. Because she was standing so very still she heard a car starting up on the other side of the hedge.

She ran through the gate just in time to see it pull out of its parking place into traffic. It was one of the new compacts with only two doors, white or some pale color that looked white after dark.

At the corner a red light brought it to a halt. Its license number was 654 2II.

She ran towards her own car. Where was her key? She had a vivid memory of shutting off the ignition, but she couldn't remember taking the key out of the car. Not that it mattered now. She kept an extra key hidden among maps in the glove compartment for just such emergencies as this.

The side street where she had left the car was one-way. She had to turn at the first corner and turn again at the second in order to get back into Beacon Street. She was just in time to slide into a space two cars behind number 654 2II.

She had thought that following another car would take all her attention, but driving is so largely a matter of reflexes that she soon found part of her mind was left free to follow another train of thought.

Was it possible that she was not following Victor at all but his lookalike, Quentin? The light from the lamppost had not been strong. She had only seen the face for a few moments. She had wanted to see Victor, and wasn't wishful seeing as common as wishful thinking?

She could not imagine any reason why Victor would visit Thereon Skinner tonight or any other night. Ever since she had first met Victor, she had been aware of his covert hostility toward his older cousin, Cornelius. That hostility had extended to Cornelius' wife, Anna. Wouldn't it also extend to Cornelius' son, Thereon?

No. Wait. Thereon was rebelling against his father and his father's way of life. A distrust of Cornelius, the head of the family, might draw two young Skinners together, and that in turn might make Cornelius angry with Victor. Parents do not love those who lead their sons or daughters away from parental standards. That was one classic cause of hostility between parents and teacher. If Cornelius saw Victor as a corrupter of his son, Victor's career at Luka, Incorporated, would not last much longer.

The car ahead was leaving Beacon Street. Following it unobserved would be harder once it left this crowded, brightly lit thoroughfare for the dark, empty back streets in this part of Brookline. Whoever was driving that other car, Victor or Quentin, would soon know he was being followed.

Marina slowed down and fell back. At each curve she rounded, she expected to find the next stretch of road empty, but her luck held. At each turning she was just in time to catch the red taillights of the car ahead flicking around the next corner.

It couldn't last. She felt no surprise at all when she rounded the fifth curve and saw that the road ahead was empty. She put on speed, but the only car she overtook was a large, black sedan with four doors. There was no sign of 654 211.

Now she had no other car to follow and no idea how to get back to Beacon Street. It was easy for a stranger to get lost in this part of Brookline after dark. There were no brightly lighted filling stations or shopping centers where she could ask her way, and she hesitated to ring the doorbell of a private house late in the evening. Many houses had no lights at all at this hour. Others had lights only on upper floors, suggesting a household preparing for bed.

She looked at her fuel gauge. If she didn't find a main road soon, she might not have enough gas to get back to Lettice's house in Lincoln.

Did she have enough money for gas? Oh, well, she had credit cards and—

She glanced at the seat beside her. Her handbag wasn't there.

But it had to be. She had had it only a little while ago. She was always careful with it, for it contained everything important—money, driver's license, registration, credit cards . . .

But tonight she had not been careful. Now she remembered. She had put the bag down beside her on the window-seat when she first began talking to Anna. It must be there still. She could not remember having seen it since.

She would have to go back to the house now and look for it.

She came to another long, dark, empty street, but at the far end of this one the fog that hung at rooftop level reflected a glow from lights below. Surely that meant a thoroughfare?

She drove toward the glow until she came to a corner busy enough to have a traffic light. She could hardly believe her luck when she saw that the road sign read: BEACON STREET.

Even now her troubles were not over for she had lost her sense of direction. Did she turn left or right to get back to the house? If she made a mistake, she might yet be stranded with an empty gas tank at an hour when most filling stations were closed.

On a clear night there would have been landmarks, the Prudential Building, the Hancock Building or that blinking red triangle at Kenmore Square, but tonight the sea mist topped all towers at the fifth floor and even at ground level familiar outlines were blurred.

If the house numbers started to diminish, it would mean that she was going the right way, toward Boston, but she still could not read them from the road at night. Once again she would have to stop at the first parking place she came to and leave the car.

She was watching for a place when she saw the house itself. To her joy the place where she had parked before was still vacant.

The inner door was just as she had left it, standing open with one of its glass panels broken. The hall was different. A crystal chandelier she had not noticed when it was unlighted and lost among shadows in the high ceiling was now ablaze with light.

Someone had been here since she left, someone who might be here still.

It was at this moment she heard footfalls in the upper hall.

If she had never seen Victor's face at the window, she would have fled. As it was, she hesitated. Could those steps be his?

If not, they might be Thereon's, and Thereon might be able to tell her where Victor was.

What other link could there be between Victor and this dreary rooming house except his cousin? Thereon might be able to explain everything now, the strange behavior of his own father, Victor's disappearance, the deceptions of Dr. Sanders, even the enigma of Quentin Yardley.

All the things that had happened to her since her accident were effects that came from causes she could neither see nor understand. She was like the men in the Platonic cave who could see only the moving shadows of reality on the wall before them and never the reality itself which was casting the shadows from behind them.

Now she saw how close to life itself that vision of a shadow-world was. The idea gave her a giddy sense of instability. For the first time she began to understand what philosophers meant when they spoke of "the shiver of the universe."

She did not call out or announce herself. She simply began to walk up the stairs, slowly, quietly, ready to turn and run for the open door if she had to.

There was no one in the upstairs hall when she got there. The whole house seemed to be clenched in a deathly stillness. Could she have been mistaken when she thought she heard footfalls? It was easy to imagine such things here, as Anna had told her.

The door to Thereon's room was open. Had she left it that way? She could not remember now.

She spoke in a voice hardly above a whisper. "Thereon? Thereon Skinner?"

The silence was unbroken.

That made her bolder.

She took a step forward and stopped at the threshold of Thereon's room. Only the lamp on the desk was lit.

By its light she saw her handbag just where she had put it down on one of the cushions that padded the window seat while she was talking to Anna.

She had picked it up and turned to leave the room when she saw something that stopped her.

A man was lying on the floor, his back toward her. His legs were hidden by the rocking chair where Anna had sat. His head was in a shadow cast by the open drop leaf of the desk. All she could see of him was a solid-looking back in a gray tweed jacket.

Men who were sleeping or drunk did not lie so still.

Something moved in the shadows beyond the lamplight. A

113

boy was staring at her. Dark slacks and yellow shirt hung loosely on his bony frame as if he had lost weight recently. His face looked adolescent, soft and easy to mold as butter, but his dark eyes were hard and brilliant as gems.

Something about him was vaguely familiar, but the unseen presence that censors all our memories would not allow her to recall his identity in this moment of shock.

"I did not kill him!" The young voice broke. "I tell you, I did not!"

"I daresay you didn't." Marina made her own voice as level as she could, hoping self-control would be contagious. "Who is he?"

"I don't know. I never saw him before in my life. Don't you know him?"

"I haven't seen his face yet."

"Take a look."

All Marina could think of then was the fact that only a little while ago she had seen Victor's face at a window in this house.

For a moment it was impossible to move. Then she reached that point where any certainty is more bearable than uncertainty.

She leaned over the body and forced herself to look down.

Even in death he was repellant. The jutting brow, scooped nose and pursed lips were like a discarded mask. There was a bullet hole in one temple, neat and almost bloodless as if it had been made by an electric drill. It seemed an absurdly small thing to have destroyed a man so large and so in love with his own vitality. It was a cruel reminder of the fragility of all human strength.

"You know him?"

"His name is Eric Sanders."

"Have you any idea what he is doing here?"

"He may have been looking for me."

"You do believe me, don't you? When I say I didn't kill him?"

Before she could answer, the night became loud with a wailing that rose and fell in plangent sobs.

"Police!" The boy gasped. "Did you call them?"

"No."

"Somebody did. I've got to get out of here."

"Why?"

"Somebody planned this. Somebody wants me to be found here."

His eyelids were stretched wide open. His eyeballs glittered as lamplight brought up their shine out of the shadows.

"If only I had my car now!"

"I've got a car around the corner," said Marina.

"Can I come with you? Please!"

He looked even younger now.

"Then hurry. Judging by that siren we have about three split seconds to get out."

Chapter Eleven

Down the hall to the back of the house, down the back stairs with clattering heels, across the kitchen, they raced all the way to the back door.

"Shall I . . . close it?" he panted.

"Yes, but . . ." She was panting, too. "Leave it unlocked . . . in case we have to . . . double back . . ."

"Then won't they think . . . ?"

"It doesn't matter."

The wail of the siren was in the next block now, but fog or traffic seemed to have stalled it there. For how long?

She was gambling on her experience of other suburbs. It was usually possible to go through back yards from one house to another, if you did not mind struggling through hedges and thorn bushes. This was the only way they could hope to reach her car in the side street without being seen by the police on Beacon Street.

She did not draw a deep breath again until they were both in the car and the doors were closed. She was turning right at the first corner, when he cried:

"One way! And you're going wrong. If anyone sees you . . ."

"No one will see us if we move fast enough." She was halfway through a tight U-turn as she spoke. "No one sees anything that you do faster than normal. That's what makes sleight of hand and subliminal advertising possible."

She turned right and right again into a street parallel with Beacon.

"By gosh, you made it!"

"We're not out of the woods yet."

"That's archaic," he said. "From the days when old-world woods were full of outlaws and wild beasts."

"And now our streets are full of outlaws and wild beasts." Marina sighed. "Soon people will be saying: 'We're not out of the streets yet!' "

She was careful to drive well below the speed limit. The attentions of the police were the last thing she wanted. Her ears were like antennae poised to catch the first tremor of a siren. Her eyes flicked to her rear-view mirror every other minute.

At Kenmore Square he said: "Have we lost them?"

"I think they never saw us. Where shall I take you now?"

He was silent.

"Well?"

"I have no place to go," he said.

"Now, really, Thereon." It slipped out before she could stop herself.

"So you know who I am?" All the panic was back in his voice.

"Of course. You're Victor's second cousin. Do you think

117

I would have taken a stranger's word that he had not killed Dr. Sanders?"

"I'm Victor's first cousin once removed. He and my father are first cousins. If Victor has a child, that child will be my second cousin. But who are you?" His voice still shivered like a tuning fork.

"I'm Marina Skinner, Victor's wife. I knew you by your portrait. I saw it in your father's Connecticut house a few days ago. You're even wearing the same yellow shirt you were when the portrait was painted, or one very like it. How about my taking you to Connecticut now? Isn't that where you would be safest? Your father's lawyers will advise you about approaching the Massachusetts police and—"

"No." The expressive young voice was no longer frightened. It was bitter. "My father and I are not on speaking terms. It's literally true that I have no place to go."

"I suppose you mean you and your father have quarreled. Such quarrels are a part of growing up."

There was something withdrawn in the quality of his silence.

Marina tried again.

"People emphasize family conflict today rather than family love, but conflict itself is a bond. You can hardly quarrel with those you care nothing about. Right now your father is probably trying to think of some way to make up his quarrel with you. Why don't you meet him halfway? He'd probably be overjoyed if you walked in tonight."

"Not my father. You don't know him."

"I've met him."

"How often?"

"Once."

"Then you don't know him at all. He hates me. He uses

118

me for his own purposes. The one thing I can never do is go home. Never."

This was more serious than she had thought.

"Won't your mother help?"

"What can she do? She can't change my father. There's no place she could hide me that he could not find. I sometimes think it would be better for everybody, including me, if I were dead."

"Nonsense!"

"I'm not just talking. I mean it. There are reasons."

"Want to tell me what they are?"

"No."

Marina did not know much about the psychology of suicide, but she did know that the suicide rate among young people had increased in the past few years. It hurt to think of any young life being thrown away for what was probably no more than some adolescent mischief, something he would outgrow in another year or so if he went on living. She could not abandon him now, so there was only one thing to do.

"I'm staying at a friend's house in Lincoln," she said. "There's plenty of room. Why don't you come there with me now and get a good night's sleep? Tomorrow you can make other plans."

"I'd like that, but I don't know why you're doing it."

"Families should hang together, and I am your cousin-in-law."

"With a father like mine, family has never meant much to me."

As Marina picked up Route 128, she said: "The fog's thinning, but I don't hear any sirens now, do you?"

"They don't always use sirens when they're following people," returned Thereon.

After that, he didn't talk much, but he spent more and more time looking behind him. Marina found her own eyes straying to the rear-view mirror a little more often than was comfortable.

There was just enough fog to make it difficult to see cars behind her, so there was really no way of telling whether there was a police car back there or not.

"Fog works both ways, doesn't it?" said Thereon. "Makes it harder for them to see us, and makes it harder for us to see them."

As they reached Route 117, there was a sudden shifting and lifting and a handful of stars broke through. Behind them, the wet road was black in the starlight and empty.

"Now we can risk stopping for gas," said Marina. "If we can find a place that is still open."

"There's one that's still lighted across the street," he answered her. "Of course lights don't always mean a place like that is open.

But it was.

"Home, free and dry!" Thereon's eyes were bright with elation. "There were moments when I thought we weren't going to make it."

Marina glanced at him sidewise. "Now are you going to tell me why you were there in Brookline?"

He grinned. "Are you going to tell me why you were there in Brookline? I'd like to know a little more about this Dr. Sanders."

"Wait till we get into the house."

There were no lights when they pulled into the driveway.

"Isn't your friend here now?"

"It doesn't look that way, does it? Lettice is a fashion model and when I left here she was off to an assignment in

New York. She said she'd be back this evening, but the fog may have held up her plane. Don't worry. She left an extra key with me."

There were switches just inside the front door for the lights in hall, living room and kitchen. Marina turned on all three.

As always, Lettice's home was spotless and uncluttered, warm and welcoming.

Thereon looked about him with dazed eyes.

"I'd forgotten there were still places like this in the world, I've been on the run so long."

"I'm hungry," said Marina. "How about club sandwiches and coffee?"

"Sounds wonderful. I'll do the bacon if you like."

Thereon seemed altogether another boy in this environment. There was no more foolishness about suicide or fathers. He broiled the bacon carefully, avoiding the extremes of burned or raw edges.

"How did you learn to do that?" asked Marina.

"One of the few things I learned at Harvard."

He took over the job of setting the table. He took pains to ask her just what mats and dishes, silver and glasses she wanted to use. When she offered him a choice of beer or wine, he chose beer, the sensible drink for late hours. He praised her hearty version of a club sandwich, which included slices of ham and cheese as well as chicken and omitted that third slice of toast drugstores use to stretch the more expensive protein ingredients.

She didn't tell him about seeing Victor's face at the window of the house in Brookline. She was not ready yet to trust him with Victor's secrets, but, at table, she did satisfy some of his curiosity about Dr. Sanders and herself.

He didn't ask questions. He just said: "Nothing surprises

121

me today." And then, after a moment: "Dr. Sanders sounds rather like my father in some ways."

While she was putting plates and silver in the dishwasher, he made the coffee.

He was not just a polite boy, he was companionable, and the more she saw of him, the more she felt uneasy about Cousin Cornelius. How could any normal father antagonize a boy like this so deeply? Thereon was worth rescuing on his own account, not just because he was Victor's cousin. A boy like this was too promising to be destroyed by a sterile conflict between parents who did not understand each other, let alone their unhappy child.

Thereon's eyelids were drooping. Every now and then he would shake his head and straighten his shoulders to keep himself awake. She thought he was exhausted emotionally as well as physically.

"You're going to bed now, young man." To her horror she realized that she was sounding like a child's nurse. "There's no reason why you should sit up for Lettice with me."

His protest was halfhearted. It took only a few moments to shoo him downstairs to the guest room she had occupied last night. There was a smaller room on this floor she could use tonight. There she would be more likely to hear Lettice when she got home.

For a while she heard Thereon moving around in the room below. The shower gushed at full force, a casement window creaked as it was opened. Now he was whistling a musical phrase in a minor key that sounded familiar, but if there were words, she could not recall them. At last silence came. He must be asleep.

The living room grew chilly. She built a fire on the hearth, got herself a last tankard of beer and looked for a distracting book on the shelves.

Lettice's landlord was obviously a sober, industrious apprentice. No Art Buchwald, no Russell Baker, no P. G. Wodehouse. All the books looked dull and all were heavy to lift, so she simply picked the lightest.

Two sofas faced each other at right angles to the hearth. Marina sat in a corner of one, near a floor lamp, and opened the book, the biography of a celebrity of yesteryear already a nobody.

In five minutes she put it down and let her memory wander to a more interesting book, David Kahn's one-man encyclopedia of cryptography.

To Kahn, encicode was simply the principle of the double safe used on submarines, a smaller safe contained within a larger safe, each with a different combination.

First you enciphered a cleartext. Then you re-enciphered that first ciphertext and got a second ciphertext. Any codebreaker who broke the outer cipher would arrive at the inner cipher and have to start his codebreaking all over again, so it would take him twice as long to get to the cleartext.

What a pity you couldn't stop the codebreaker right there at the halfway stage by making him believe that the first ciphertext was the cleartext. . . .

Or could you?

What made a codebreaker believe he had reached a cleartext?

The coherence of the text itself. The mathematical chances of getting a coherent text by accident were astronomical, so he assumed that any coherent text had to be the cleartext.

But did it?

An idea began to boil and bubble in her brain.

Suppose . . . just suppose . . . that a ciphertext could be

made coherent and used as a second step in encicou. Then it would be a decoy text, fooling the codebreaker so he would stop his analysis right there and never go on to the real cleartext?

Could this be done?

How about a running incoherent key with each letter chosen in a manner as totally random as a throw of the dice?

Instead of ciphertext being determined by the interaction of key and cleartext, wouldn't key be determined by the interaction of cleartext and ciphertext?

Couldn't you then control the pairing of letters and letter substitutes so you could produce any words you wanted in the decoy text?

Impossible? Crazy?

Of course. And therefore exactly the sort of thing that Victor would love to do. If he had, the oracular words of the French song were not open code at all. They were the decoy text in a new two-step cipher, and somewhere beyond them, in the jungle of incoherent alphabets, the secret cleartext still lay snugly hidden.

How could you break a cipher like that?

There were no instruction books. She would have to wing it.

She found a memo pad in the kitchen and came back to her seat by the fire. Her pen flew over the paper, trying to keep pace with her thoughts, but no muscular action can catch up with thought, which makes quantum leaps in thousandths of a second. There were moments when whole complexes of related ideas slid out of her mind before she had time to write them down, even in her own personal speedwriting.

An hour passed before she was ready to test her theory.

Then once again she made her Saint Cyr slide rule, cutting out two paper strips of unequal length, writing the typewriter alphabet once on the shorter or index strip and writing the English frequency alphabet twice on the longer or slide strip.

The shorter strip was easier to move, so she picked a hypothetical first key letter, G, at random in the slide alphabet and moved the index until that G was under the first letter in the index alphabet, Q. She then found the first letter of the ciphertext, C, on the slide and looked at the letter above it on the index, which turned out to be B.

Could that letter be the first letter of the real cleartext which Victor had hidden behind two ciphertexts?

It wasn't. By the time she had got to the tenth possible clear letter she had nothing coherent. Oh, well . . . she had not expected to win on the first throw, but, if she went on playing alphabetic roulette, wasn't there a chance she might extract some set of coherent syllables or bigrams that suggested a mathematical frequency approach?

She moved the index to and fro and jotted down possible cleartext letters as they came.

Suddenly a small pulse began to beat in her throat.

There is no excitement quite like the breaking of a cipher. It is a peculiarly exhilarating form of pattern recognition under stress.

Was a coherent word building now?

C . . . O . . . P . . .

L . . . U . . . S . . .

United States? Was that L just a null?

L . . . V . . . X . . . E . . . Q . . .

She threw down her pen.

Damn and damn and damn.

Her eyes were sandy, her mouth parched, her hair was

tangled, and all in vain. She had failed.

The letters, L V X E Q, were not coherent at all.

She had been sitting still so long that one foot had gone to sleep. The biggest log on the hearth had burned through the middle and broken in half. Time for bed.

She banked the fire and put up the fire screen, but left the hall light on for Lettice. She was so tired she tumbled into bed without brushing her hair or cleaning her teeth.

She was half-asleep when there floated before her closed eyes an image of the upper left-hand quadrant of a clock. The clock was square with a blue face. The symbols for the four hours were not numbers. They were large, round black dots. The hour hand was solid blue. The minute hand was an outline in white. The position of the hands told her that it was midnight.

She opened her eyes and switched on a light. The little clock on the bedside table read twenty-five minutes after eleven, so her dream clock was fast.

Where had that image come from? She could not recall ever having seen a square blue clock. Could you dream about something you had never seen in reality? Or was the blue clock a composite of all the clocks she had ever seen since she was born?

And yet . . . Had she seen a blue clock not so long ago? Where?

It came to her at last. This afternoon, in Thereon's room in Brookline, she had seen the *Bulletin of the Atomic Scientists* with the famous Doomsday Clock on the cover.

The magazine was founded by scientists who had worked on the Manhattan Project as a protest against the drift toward nuclear war. The clock had first appeared on the cover in 1947. Whenever the danger of war came closer, the hands moved closer to midnight. Whenever the danger seemed less, the hands moved farther from midnight.

In 1953 they had stood at two minutes to midnight, and how many people realized that then? In 1963 they stood at eleven minutes to midnight. Now, on the copy in Thereon's rooms, they were standing at nine minutes to midnight, but in her dream they had stood exactly at midnight itself.

Only then did she identify the air that Thereon had been whistling as he prepared for bed. It was the musical phrase that went with the words: *Midnight has already struck . . .*

Had Thereon simply picked up the song from Victor? Or did Thereon know something about the ciphertext?

Of course not. Who would tell a boy of twenty about such things? There was nothing to worry about. Midnight was not going to strike on the Doomsday Clock or any other cosmic timepiece. The world had lived for a generation since Hiroshima. The survival instinct was too stubborn to permit species suicide. Human beings were not going to throw away something it had taken four million years to build.

Still she could not sleep.

Again she looked at the bedside clock.

Midnight and the world was still here.

Too late for a drink or too early?

Whichever it was, she was going to have one.

She put on her dressing gown and slippers and went into the kitchen.

It was at the front of this modern house. She had just reached it when she heard a car surge into the driveway with a squeal of tires.

The kitchen windows were too high for her to look out. An architect's mistake. In these days people like to see who's on the doorstep before they open the door.

127

She was hesitating between advancing or waiting for the bell to ring, when she heard the reassuring sound of a key in the lock.

"Lettice!" Marina cried out joyfully as she ran into the hall. The door burst open. She stood still.

"Victor . . ."

III - EVERYWHERE

III · EVERY WHERE

Chapter Twelve

In that first moment of shock her vision was a moving camera eye flashing from one point to another in such incoherent sequence that details blurred in a freakish montage: the pearls of water the fog had left on his dark hair, the dampness that streaked his pale raincoat with a deeper shade of tan, his look of utter astonishment as his eyes met hers.

"Marina!"

His kiss left her no doubt that this was Victor.

After a while she stirred in his arms.

"Where have you been? What happened to you?"

"Everything."

He held her a little closer. She looked up into his face and saw lines that had not been there before. Did he know that the baby was lost? She could not bear to tell him now during these first few moments of being together again after so many days.

"Marina, did you know that I actually saw your accident? I was watching from the top of the hill when that other car came out of nowhere and hit yours. A white car with a black top. I ran down the hill. By the time I got to the foot of the drive, it was gone. The police never found it. They say it could be anywhere by this time at the bottom of a lake or halfway to South America. We'll never know who was driving it."

"It was a man," said Marina. "I saw his head and shoulders."

"But not his face?"

"Not his face."

"I spent that night at the clinic. Dr. Sanders let me see you next morning."

"Why don't I remember that?"

"You were still unconscious, but Sanders said you were out of danger. He urged me to keep an appointment I had with Cornelius, so I did. Worst mistake I ever made for he never let me see you again, damn him. He kept saying that you would never recover your memory if you saw me before you were ready. He wouldn't let me telephone you or even write to you. And by that time I had got myself in such a hellish situation that I didn't dare go near you anyway for fear of involving you in my own danger. I did risk telephoning the clinic every day and—

"Today, when I finally took a chance and went to the clinic, the head nurse told me that you were an unruly patient who had left suddenly and she had no idea where you were now. I was frantic. I thought you were being held as a hostage somewhere for Project Vortex."

"What is Project Vortex?"

"The less you know about that the better. I called Anna. She couldn't tell me where you were. I tried to call Lettice here. No one answered this telephone. I went to Brookline. The police were in charge. Thereon had disappeared and Dr. Sanders had been killed. I risked going home then, but you weren't there. This was the only other place I could think of where you might be. You can imagine how I felt when the door opened and I saw you. As for Thereon—"

"He's here, downstairs. Asleep."

"Thank God for that!" Victor's sigh was windy, as if he had run a long way.

"He's in danger, too?"

"It began with Thereon."

"I want to hear all about everything that's happened to you," she said. "But first I'm going to get you something to eat. You look hungry and tired and cold. Why don't you go into the living room and build up the fire while I see what there is in the kitchen?"

She found cold roast beef and bread, cheese and fruit. She made instant coffee and added a bottle of brandy to the tray she took into the living room.

Victor had brought the dying fire to life again. Now he stood close to the blaze, studying one of the work sheets she had left scattered on the floor. He looked up with a grin.

"Don't worry. I haven't messed up your unique filing system. Just picked up one page. Where did you get this ciphertext?"

"It arrived at our house in an envelope addressed to you in your own handwriting." She poured coffee for both of them and added brandy, "It was stolen and opened by a man who said his name was Quentin Yardley. I got it back from him by a trick."

"So old Quent has been nosing around."

"You know him?"

"Only too well."

"He said he worked for the CCIE, but they never heard of him. Do you know whom he works for?"

"Oh, yes." Victor's eyes were bright. "I give you one guess."

"Cousin Cornelius?"

"Got it in one. Quent is stupid. For a man. He would have made a very good dog. Unswerving loyalty and instant obedience. Begs nicely, too, and rarely makes a mess on the rug. I'm sure he salivates whenever anybody says 'Luka, Incorporated.' Pavlov would have loved him. I don't."

"So I gather." It hardly seemed the ideal moment to tell Victor that Quentin had been impersonating Victor himself.

"Was he looking for me at our house?"

"Probably. He said he came to see if your mail was still being delivered there, but he behaved as if his real concern was keeping me from going to the police about your disappearance."

"And I bet it was. Cornelius wouldn't want the publicity."

Victor was making himself an enormous sandwich out of whole wheat bread, beef and cheese.

"Quentin seemed to think you'd disappeared on a trip to Iran."

"That same old trip that I never made, but I suppose he had to explain my disappearance to you somehow."

"He hinted that you'd been leaking Luka trade secrets."

"To whom?"

"A foreign company, Société Anonyme Mazda. Ever hear of them?"

"Luka's chief competitor. Quite capable of bribing or blackmailing anybody, but they've never made me any offers."

Victor picked up the ciphertext again. "Get anywhere with this?"

134

His question was too casual. Why was her answer so important to him? Why didn't he say so openly?

"I got a first sentence in clear," she answered. "MIDNIGHT HAS ALREADY STRUCK. After that it was easy because I knew the rest had to be part of the same song. Then I began to wonder if the song itself was open code, the second step in a two-step cipher. Was it?"

"A second step? Yes, but not open code."

"Hasn't the song anything to do with the Doomsday Clock on the cover of the *Bulletin of the Atomic Scientists?*"

"There's probably a relation. I must have picked the song to use in the cipher because I was thinking about the Doomsday Clock, but I didn't use the song as open code."

"Then your cipher has me stymied. I never got beyond that second step except for one idea that was just too wild to work."

"And what was that?"

"It suddenly came to me how wonderful it would be if you could make the second ciphertext in a two-step cipher as coherent as a cleartext. Then most codebreakers would assume they had reached the only cleartext there was and stop right there without even trying to go on and break the second step. Has it ever been used before?"

"Only twice as far as I know. It would be used more often if it wasn't for smart people like you who guess that the apparent cleartext is really a double encipherment. You're too smart." He kissed her.

"How on earth did you do it?"

"With an incoherent running key and the choice of each key letter made arbitrarily to fit the ciphertext which I already knew."

"Oh, Victor, I thought of that very thing, but when I analyzed the words of the song as if they were ciphertext, I just got gibberish."

"You probably didn't stick with it long enough. Remember the opening sentence in Parker Hitt's famous manual? 'Success in dealing with unknown ciphers is measured by these four things in the order named: perseverance, careful methods of analysis, intuition, and luck.' Perseverance is the first. Come here."

He switched on the lamp beside the sofa where she had sat earlier this evening. He put his arm around her and drew her down on the sofa beside him, and how much pleasanter that was than sitting there alone.

The shaded light from the lamp struck up at his face from below, emphasizing the new lines there by filling them with shadow. For a moment he looked the way he would look twenty years from now. Then he smiled and the years fell away.

"Look, darling. Let's take the third line in the last stanza to work on. In the first ciphertext it reads:

"RFBIJ EMVOR NJHWQ QDZDI ACOW.

"And here is the result of the first analysis, step one:

"MIDNI GHTHA SALRE ADYST RUCK.

"Is that a cleartext? No. It's a ciphertext disguised as a cleartext which I call a decoytext. So you analyse it exactly as you would any other ciphertext. That is step two and it gives you . . . what?"

"All it gave me was COPLU SLVXE Q . . . I stopped right there at that Q because it is so obviously gibberish."

"Is it?"

He used one of her pens to underline the first three letters.

"So those letters spell COP," she said. "But the next letters

136

are LUSLVXEQ and they don't spell anything."

"How about this?"

He drew a vertical line between the O and the P and another between the S and the L.

She frowned. "CO . . . PLUS?"

"Think, Marina. What is the mathematical probability of getting a word like PLUS in a cipher analysis by accident?"

"Enormous, I'm sure, though the word COW did show up in the third line of the first ciphertext and I'm sure that was chance. Anyway the preceding letters here, CO, are meaningless and—"

"Are they?"

"Commanding officer?"

"No, something chemical."

"Oh, carbon monoxide. Then I did break this after all?"

"You broke it without knowing it. You must have been tired. If you had gone on for one more letter you would have got a U after a Q and realized that could hardly be accident, since Q is always followed by U in English text."

Marina read aloud, looking over his shoulder. "CO PLUS LVX EQU . . . Oh, I see. EQUALS DFG SQUARE."

A formula of some kind. That might explain why he had not used nulls in the ciphertext. He wanted to keep the formula visibly uncluttered, so he could refer to each part separately and quickly, if he had to.

"But what about LVX and DFG?" asked Marina. "They're just as cryptic in cleartext as in ciphertext."

"Not to anyone familiar with the new laser technology," answered Victor. "It has a jargon all its own. HPPG means high-powered, pulsed gas laser. XL is X-ray laser. GR is gamma-ray laser. IIB is independent ionization beam. IPD is iodine photo dissolution. And so on."

"Laser?" She tasted the word. "Isn't that something they use in eye surgery?"

"And when they operate on cancer of the windpipe, but it has other uses, less benign." He crumpled the sheet of paper and tossed it into the fire. It flashed into flame, then died to ash, first black, then white.

"We'd better burn all this stuff," he said.

"Am I never going to see the whole cleartext?"

His only answer was to take her face between his hands and kiss her lips gently.

"Why can't I?"

"You know enough already. Perhaps too much."

"About what? Lasers?"

He weighed his answer, then picked his way among his next words gingerly as if they were explosives.

"Did I ever mention something called Project Vortex to you before?"

"No, you never talked shop at home."

"I'll have to now. Vortex is a new kind of laser weapon. This ciphertext is the only written record of the design and manufacturing process that still exists. Of all the people who have read it in clear, only two are now alive."

"Who are the two?"

"Thereon and me. You look as if you don't believe me."

"It's a little hard to believe."

"Why?"

"I thought this was the age of teamwork in all research. I thought the individual genius, like Darwin or Pasteur, went out with the bustle. In technical journals most of the reports I see are signed by ten or fifteen names. Even when somebody wins a Nobel prize, he's usually described as the leader of a group."

138

"And he usually is, but not always, even today. Five men worked on Vortex. No more. It would have been hard to keep the thing so secret if there had been more. It started out as pure research. No one thought anything practical would come of it. They used workshops only for testing theories. It was too early to build permanent models. Temporary models were destroyed after each test for security reasons. So, when the potential of the thing was finally realized, Luka's most valuable property existed only in the brains of five men."

A premonition hit her.

"Why do you speak of them in the past tense?"

"Because all five are dead now."

"Sabotage?"

"No evidence of anything so tidy. It was probably an honest, inadvertent blunder, made by an underpaid clerk in our transportation department. 'Oversight' was his own word for it. He let all five scientists working on Vortex go to Iran on the same plane, one of Luka's private jets."

"And it crashed?"

"In the mountains near Teheran. We'll never know whether it was sabotage or not. Everything burned—plane, men, documents. Perhaps it was just Murphy's Law: if anything can go wrong, it will.

"Thereon and I were the only people left who really knew anything about the Vortex formula. That is changing our whole lives."

"There's been nothing in the papers about a Luka jet crashing in Iran, and nothing about a new laser weapon."

"You bet there hasn't. Cornelius has a special relationship with Iran and a damned good security department. No word of that crash ever got out of Iran. He also has a press relations department so efficient that you hardly ever see mention of military lasers in mass media. Only in technical journals or some feisty little newsletter like *Washington Watch*. Even they don't know about Vortex."

"Victor, what is a laser?"

"The word is an acronym for Light Amplification by Stimulated Emission of Radiation."

"Translate, please."

"You might call it a highly focussed beam of light. The work *luka* is Old Slavonic for a beam or ray."

"Would anyone commit murder for what is, after all, just another weapon?"

She was surprised by the look of sadness in his eyes. His answer came slowly.

"The Laser is more than that. Its range is pure science fiction. It can bounce a signal off reflectors left on the moon by astronauts. That's nearly half a million miles from earth. It can do everything a nuclear bomb can do: generate shock waves in gases liquids and solids; create particle beams and explode wires. It vaporizes steel or iron in the tiny moment between one millionth and one billionth of a second. It can burn a hole in a diamond. You may imagine its effect on the human body.

"I don't think I want to."

"In spite of all these goodies, ordinary lasers have one tactical drawback: they can travel only in a straight line."

"Like Chinese devils? They can't fly around corners?"

"Exactly. They can't be bent or curved to go over or under or around anything. Or rather they couldn't until a few months ago. Now Vortex lasers can. Ordinary lasers can wipe out a full-scale missile attack from land bases or submarines in a few minutes, but only if the missiles come in at the right level and angle. Vortex lasers can be bent or twisted or

140

curved to meet any missiles anywhere."

"The perfect weapon?"

"Except for one strategic drawback: it does not cause fallout."

"Aw, shucks!"

"All right, my sweet, have your little sick joke. Then ask yourself one question: what has prevented all-out war since Hiroshima and Nagasaki?"

The laughter went out of Marina's eyes. "Fallout?"

"What else? Fallout was our guardian angel and now it's gone."

"The very thing we've been praying for."

"Beware the curse of an answered prayer. Remember Jacobs' old story, *The Monkey's Paw?* The nuclear age is coming to an end sooner than we thought. An arms limitation treaty that does not mention lasers is just window dressing now."

They lay together on the sofa silently for a while watching the fire. He was the first to speak.

"You and I have lost our first child in an accident. That's hard enough to bear. How would we feel if it had been a deliberate act of war?"

"So you know?"

"Dr. Sanders told me the last time I saw him. He used it as another argument against my seeing you."

She turned around in his arms so she could look into his eyes.

"You've changed."

"Have I?" He smiled. "I was brought up in a fool's paradise, Marina. Now I've been up against reality. I could never go back to that paradise, even if I wanted to, but I don't want to."

141

Now, at last, everything was in the open again and she could talk him as freely as she always had before. It was pure delight to be able to talk once more to the one man who would never misunderstand her or misjudge her.

"I have so many questions to ask you. I don't know where to begin. Have you any idea who deposited that fifty thousand in your account?"

"No, but I can guess why it was deposited. To tempt me or to compromise me. Probably by a Mazda agent. This has been done before. It's hard to convince anyone that you don't know the provenance of a large sum of money in your account."

"Why did Quentin Yardley help me to get out of the clinic?"

"Quent takes no action that does not protect Cousin Cornelius or advance his interest. I would guess that Quent thought you, as my wife, knew something about Vortex, and he was afraid Dr. Sanders might get information out of you."

"Then why didn't he say so?"

"Vortex is top secret. Quent didn't know how much you knew and he didn't trust you because he doesn't trust me now I've broken with Cornelius."

"How did you and Thereon get drawn into all this? You're not a scientist. He's only a college dropout."

"Cornelius started it. I'd heard rumors about Vortex that worried me ever since we came to Boston, but that was all until the day of your accident. Cornelius was in Boston that day. He called me and said he wanted me to go to Iran on what he called a 'diplomatic mission.' I tried to get out of it, but Cornelius doesn't like to be crossed. He cut up rough."

"So you went?"

"Hell, no! I wasn't going to have you waking up in that clinic and asking for me while I was out of the country."

"Your office told me on the telephone that you had gone."

"Orders from Cornelius, no doubt, to cover up the truth."

"Which was?"

"I told Cornelius exactly what he could do with my damned job and walked out on him. Thereon heard about it and came to see me at home next day. He wanted me to share the Vortex responsibility with him. He gave me a copy of the formula to study. I enciphered it for safekeeping and he jotted down his Brookline address on the wrong side so we could keep in touch.

"It was then he told me the truth about my so-called 'diplomatic mission.' I had assumed that Cornelius had a contract with the Pentagon or the Navy. Thereon opened my eyes. Cornelius has no contract with anybody yet. He is trying to sell Vortex to the highest bidder in the international market. My diplomacy in Teheran would have been simply to start the bidding like any other shill or huckster."

"But wouldn't Vortex make any nation who owned it exclusively master of the world?"

"Of course. That's why it's worth so much money."

"And Cornelius doesn't care who buys it?"

"Why should he? His interests are truly multinational. He really is one of those men who have 'no conscience and no country.' And, indeed, no species. You won't catch Cornelius lying awake at night worrying about the future of humanity."

"What are you and Thereon going to do?"

"We haven't worked it out yet. When we realized that agents from both Luka and Mazda were after us, we holed up in Brookline. We lived the way the French underground used to call *sans soleil.* We only went out after dark, like cockroaches.

"The only thing we could agree upon was what we'd like to do when it was all over: go abroad. It was a wretched time. Thereon was unhappy about his break with his father and I was unhappy because I was so worried about you. I couldn't even decide to go abroad until you were well enough to travel.

"I missed my job. I even missed my own car. I had to borrow Thereon's, the one I'm driving tonight. That macabre old house where we were didn't help either. Something was wrong with the front door. It wouldn't lock unless you slammed it and half the time I forgot to. Anybody could have walked in at any moment. Apparently Dr. Sanders did."

"What does Thereon himself want to do about Vortex now?"

Before Victor could answer, there was a sound of stumbling on the stairs in the hall that led up from the floor below. Thereon appeared in the archway, hair tousled, eyelids puffy, one cheek creased and red where he must have lain upon it.

He had chosen to sleep in his shirt and slacks, and they were now more crushed than ever. He stood on bare feet, his eyes blinking in the bright light.

Marina thought: He looks like a Babe in the Woods who has just discovered what the Wicked Uncle is up to.

"My room's just under this one," he said. "I can't help hearing you talk. I thought you ought to know it."

"You're still asleep, Ronnie," said Victor. "Go back to bed."

Thereon frowned. "I'm not going to let you drag Marina any further into this."

144

Victor cocked an eyebrow at Marina and murmured: "You've made a conquest." He said to Thereon: "I'm not dragging Marina into anything. She dragged herself into this by getting hold of the ciphertext. Why are you so upset?"

"I've just thought of something," said Thereon. "It came to me when I first woke up. It all began with her accident long before she ever saw or heard of a ciphertext."

"What began?" Victor was growing impatient, but Thereon's attention was still on the girl.

"Marina, I don't know whether it has anything to do with Vortex or not, but I'm convinced now that someone is trying to kill you. The accident was the first attempt. There may be others."

Chapter Thirteen

Victor turned to look at Thereon.

"Are you crazy?"

Marina sat still, looking down the long vista of memories that suddenly unfolded before her. Until now her situation had seemed to her like an unsolved picture puzzle, a jumble of pieces jigsawed in random shapes and scattered across a table, no edges meshing, no lines continuous, no colors matching.

Now whole clusters of tangential lines and eccentric colors leapt into realignment here and there, forming partially coherent fragments obviously part of an overall design she could not yet see.

"He's not crazy," she said to Victor. "It's like breaking a cipher. The pattern has been there all along but Thereon has got the wrong victim. It's you that someone is trying to kill."

"Me?"

"Let's go back to the beginning. Whose car was I driving when the accident happened?"

"Mine, but—"

"Darling Victor, don't you realize that the apparent accident to me could have been an attempt to murder you? It was a few minutes after sunset, the half hour before people are legally obliged to switch on headlights. In that twilight it would have been hard to see who was driving. Suppose the other driver assumed that you were driving just because it was your car? "Have you forgotten? That was the day Thereon told you about Vortex, the day you had your first clash with Cornelius."

Victor turned back to Thereon. "You're serious about this?"

"I was never more serious, but I still think Marina was the intended victim. What better way to put pressure on you than an act of violence against her? Like saying: We got your wife this time. We'll get you next time, unless . . ."

"Unless what?" Victor's voice was sharp.

Thereon answered with a sigh. "I'm afraid all roads lead to my father now."

"What about Mazda?" said Marina.

Victor was shaken but he was still in opposition. "Let's put this in plain English, Ronnie. Are you accusing your own father of attempted murder? Are you saying that he tried to overcome my objections to his policy at Luka by a physical threat to Marina or me?"

"He wouldn't see it that way," said Thereon. "A thing like that goes down through a chain of command so long and tortuous that Father might be able to convince himself he had no part in it. He'd tell himself that someone like Quentin misunderstood him or exceeded instructions. Indeed it might be the driver of the other car who made the actual decision. Then Father could say to himself truthfully: I had nothing to do with it."

"Or he could wash his hands and ask: What is truth?"

147

Victor was pacing the floor as he always did when he was worried, but he managed to laugh. "Wouldn't a gang contract be simpler? And more nearly anonymous?"

But Thereon took this seriously. "That's another possibility. Gangsters use traffic accidents for their public executions. It's the one form of killing they can spread all over newspapers and television safely because it's so difficult to prove intent. A car is now recognized legally as a lethal weapon."

Victor paused in his pacing. "What about Dr. Sanders? Is this why he tried so hard to make Marina believe her memory of the other car was a delusion?"

"That fits," said Thereon. "But why did he keep telling her she had never been pregnant?"

"I think he was trying to break down my faith in myself," said Marina. "And he nearly succeeded. I was beginning to doubt my own sanity when Quentin Yardley got me out of there. I don't like to think what might have happened if I had had to stay there any longer."

"And it was only after you pretended to accept his version of what had happened that he let you go with Yardley," said Victor. "Someone gave Sanders the job of turning a crime into an accident by inducing amnesia in you. Sanders was using psychiatry to maim, not to heal."

"I have a question," said Marina. "If the driver of the other car had been caught, what would have been the charge against him?"

"Something like attempted homicide with a lethal weapon, to wit, a car, resulting in bodily harm," said Victor. "That's if you could prove intent."

"What about the death of the unborn baby?"

"State laws vary as to when an embryo must be considered

148

alive and human, but I doubt if that aspect of the case would enhance the defendant's chances in any state. Certainly not if it was a jury trial. Why do you want to know, Marina?"

"I'm wondering if the penalty for the fake accident is harsh enough to give the killer a motive for a second killing to cover up the first?"

"In other words," said Victor, "you're wondering if Sanders was killed because he knew too much. I think he was, but there's something else I can't understand. How did a psychiatrist of his standing get mixed up in such a squalid business? What was there in it for him?"

"Nothing emotional in his case," said Marina. "He wasn't human enough to have emotions."

"And it could hardly be psychosis," added Thereon. "His colleagues would have caught on by this time. So what does that leave? Ideology? Fanaticism?"

"He was too sophisticated for that," said Marina. "There just isn't anything."

"Oh, yes, there is." Victor looked from Marina to Thereon and back to Marina. "Haven't either of you got it yet? Espionage."

"You mean industrial espionage?" said Thereon.

"Of course. That's the only kind that pays and rarely involves a death penalty."

Marina was bewildered. "Are you saying that Dr. Sanders was an international industrial spy like Quentin Yardley?"

"Exactly." Victor stopped pacing the floor and sat down beside her. "Didn't I tell you about Luka's chief competitor, Société Anonyme Mazda, subsidiary of Durand Moselle, incorporated in France and financed in Iran? Doesn't the name Mazda suggest anything?"

"Only an electric light bulb when I was a child."

"Ahura Mazda was the Iranian God of Light, Wisdom and Virtue. Mazda et Cie does not deal much in wisdom or virtue, but they've been carrying on a passionate love affair with one type of laser for several years."

"It's a carbon dioxide laser with an independent ionization beam," Thereon rattled off the words as if he had known them by heart from babyhood, and Marina remembered Anna saying that he had total recall.

"But all Mazda lasers travels in a straight line," Victor went on. "So Mazda would sell its corporate soul to Ahriman, the Iranian devil, to get its paws on our little trinket, Vortex, which bends and bounces through space like a ballerina."

"And I suppose these Mazda people recruited Sanders long ago before he was successful?"

"Oh, no. After he was successful. A generation ago you picked your spy and then found him a cover. Today we're smarter. We pick the man who already has an unimpeachable cover and turn him into a spy by exploiting some flaw in his temperament or some scandal in his past. You see when the cover is created before the spy, you can't break the cover because it's real. No fake identity, no forged passport, no big repuation that can't be backed up in academe or *Who's Who*. He's just what he claims to be."

"Sanders fills the bill nicely," added Thereon. "For forty or fifty years he probably led a life that was irreproachable on the surface. Then Mazda saw his possibilities and probed until they found his weaknesses, like a dentist probing an apparently sound tooth for the decay that only shows up on X-rays. His clinic alone would make him enormously useful to them, a place where they could hold people and work on them indefinitely."

150

"He wouldn't have had a chance to work on me if I hadn't been taken to the clinic after the accident," said Marina. "Who suggested that? The police? Or someone else?"

"Damned if I remember now," said Victor. "It was the nearest place, of course, and I've been hearing about it ever since we moved to Lincoln."

"Maybe that's why she was injured in Lincoln," suggested Thereon. "So she would be taken there."

Victor rose to put another log on the fire, then turned to face the other two, his back to the hearth.

"We haven't made much progress, have we?" he said. "We don't even know whether the intended victim was Marina or me. We don't know who killed Sanders. We don't even know why Sanders was in Brookline."

"I know," said Thereon. "He was looking for me. He wanted Vortex for Mazda. He suspected I knew more about it than I admitted. He was tired of offering me money. Next time he would have used force. I would never have gone back to that Brookline house if I had known he had traced me there."

There was a pause that grew into a silence.

Then Victor spoke. "We're going to turn it over to our own government, Ronnie, and let them deal with your father's private adventures in public policy, as they see fit."

"No government must have it." Thereon rose to face Victor. "It must be destroyed tonight, now, while we still have the chance to do so."

"Wouldn't it be better to give it to all governments?" said Marina. "Wouldn't it be neutralized if no one had it exclusively?

Victor adopted an elder brother tone. "You're both being

childish. Ronnie, you can't destroy this thing tonight or any other night."

"Why not?"

"Because other researchers will discover it again at any moment. Why do you think Darwin and Wallace discovered evolution at the same time? Because ideas are in the air during certain periods in history. Their seeds may be planted in the past, but they come to fruition when their time is ripe, and you can't stop that. You can only delay it."

"Then let's delay it as long as we can," said Marina. "I've often heard you say that a cipher can't hide a military secret forever, but it can delay discovery long enough to change the course of history."

"We might have done that ten years ago. It's too late now. Laser research has gone too far. Midnight has already struck."

Thereon walked over to the big window that overlooked the meadow and the lake. The curtains were not drawn but all that could be seen outside now was the black sky and the blurred glitter of the Milky Way, our home galaxy.

He turned again to face Victor and Marina.

"There are millions of people out there who would like to stop this new laser if they knew about it. They don't, but we three do and at this moment we three have the power to stop it. Why don't we? Do you realize the last seventy-five years have been the most violent in history? That those years have seen the deaths of nearly one hundred million people in wars? Do you really want to turn this new laser over to the human wolf pack?"

"Suppose you deny it to your country and another country gets it?"

"The old, old argument, but it isn't going to work this time."

"Why not?"

"Because for the first time in history it's up to one man to make the decision. Me."

Marina stared at him. "What on earth do you mean, Ronnie?"

"Don't tell her," said Victor. "Don't tell anybody."

"Look here, Victor, you can't order me around."

"Can't I?"

"No, and don't try."

Marina thought she could hear echoes of boyish confrontations long ago when Victor, as the elder, must always have had the advantage in height and weight.

Now he was trying to be tactful. "I want to protect you, Ronnie. Don't you realize you're putting your own life in danger?"

"The only thing that should matter to either of us now is the life of our species," said Thereon.

They had been talking so loudly that none of them had heard the approach of a car. Now, without warning, the doorbell rang. A sharp note, strident as an alarm.

Marina looked at the clock. Three in the morning. Who called at such an hour? She remembered old stories of the Gestapo and new stories of roving adolescents high on heroin. Any unexpected visitor at such an hour created a feeling of menace.

The two men were as startled as she. Through the archway they could all see a bright light piercing the darkness outside the kitchen windows.

Victor's height made it just possible for him to look out. "Damn!"

The bell rang again, louder and longer this time.

"Who is it?" whispered Marina.

"Cornelius."

Chapter Fourteen

Dismay? Consternation? What was the right word for the long look Thereon and Victor exchanged? Could it be fear?

For a son to live in fear of a father seemed impossibly medieval in the context of a society still passing through a revolution in family relationships. It was even more archaic to think of Victor living in fear of an older cousin. Yet the moment the word fear entered Marina's mind it seemed the only word to match that hopeless look that passed between the cousins.

"He mustn't find you here," said Victor. "Go downstairs again. Don't make a sound. Don't turn on a light. He has no way of knowing you are here. We'll see that he has no chance to guess."

"There's no way out down there. If he tries to come down, you'll stop him?"

"We'll stop him."

"And the ciphertext?"

"Safest with you now." Victor folded the single sheet of paper and pushed it down in the pocket of Thereon's shirt. He gave Thereon a little push toward the stairs. All hostility between them had melted away. They were allies the moment they were confronted with Cornelius.

The doorbell pealed again.

Victor waited until the light on the stairs went out and they heard a door close on the floor below.

Then he moved toward the front door.

"I'm not even dressed." Marina looked down at her quilted-cotton dressing gown. "What are you going to tell him?"

"There's no time to plan. You'll just have to take your cues from me."

Victor threw the door open.

"Why, Cousin Cornelius! What a surprise!"

The seasoning of irony was delicate, as if it had come from the hand of a master chef, and then he spoiled it.

"Do you know it's three o'clock in the morning?"

Surely that was overdoing it.

"And yet you have not retired." Cornelius' voice was as gentle as his smile. "Good evening, Marina. Or should I say good morning?"

He gave her no chance to answer. He glanced back over his shoulder and said: "You may wait outside."

Was he speaking to a chauffeur? Or to someone who had a closer relation to him? Impossible to tell by his tone of voice. No matter whom he was speaking to, he always put a distance between himself and everyone else.

"How did you know we were here?" demanded Victor.

"We tried every other place we could think of first. It was Yardley who suggested this."

Still standing on the threshold, he allowed his glance to wander around the room for a moment.

Then he spoke quietly

"Where is Thereon?"

"I have no idea," said Victor.

Now Cornelius came forward into the room. He was wearing a homburg hat, gray suede gloves and an overcoat with a velvet collar, clothes so unfamiliar today, even in conservative Lincoln, that they made him look like a time traveler from another century.

He took off his hat and laid it on a chair. He peeled off his gloves and dropped them in the hat. Victor helped him off with the coat but did not hang it in a closet. He merely folded it and put it down on the back of a chair.

Was this a hint that he did not expect Cornelius to stay long? Marina suspected that Cornelius would ignore any hint that did not fit his own plans.

She roused herself to play hostess. "Won't you sit down? Would you like coffee? Or a drink?"

"Nothing, thank you."

Cornelius was perfectly polite, but the distance between himself and others was still there. He took out a modest, leather cigarette case and lit a cigarette as if he could not go without one for even a few moments. It was another thing about him that belonged to the mores of the twenties, the golden age of the smoker when no one had yet linked cigarettes and cancer.

Marina noticed again how large his head seemed in relation to his puny body. That, even more than his hunched shoulders and bowed neck, was what gave one the impression of a humpback though there was no hump.

All her first impressions of him were being confirmed now. His face had lost none of its unhealthy pallor. He had probably looked this way for thirty years and would go on looking this way until he died.

They were sitting in the long end of the L-shaped room.

157

The last of the fire was dying in the embers on the hearth, but Victor made no move to replenish it. Around the coner, in the short arm of the L, Victor's tray and glass and plate were still standing on the dining table, a long oval of natural teak.

Cornelius sat facing the big window that overlooked the lake. His glance went up now to an array of stars like the lights of a distant city.

"Have you ever stopped to think what night really is?" he asked.

Victor shook his head impatiently.

Marina found herself listening for any whisper of sound that might betray the presence belowstairs. The smile she turned on Cornelius was a muscular effort and probably looked it.

But Cornelius was not going to be hurried.

"Night is the time when we turn our backs on our domestic hearth, the sun, and look outward with nothing between us and infinity. If you think of it that way, it is frightening."

"But you are not easily frightened." There was an an edge to Victor's voice.

"No, fortunately. A frightened man does not survive long in this world. I wish I could teach Thereon that."

Marina wondered: Does he know or guess that Thereon is downstairs and can't get out? Is that why he's taking his time? To wear us down?

Cornelius drew smoke into his lungs, savored it for a moment, then exhaled slowly.

"You know why I have come here tonight?"

"I can guess."

"Either you or Thereon has the only written copy of the Vortex process still in existence. It's mine and I want it.

158

Quentin says it's in cipher now. I want the key to the cipher as well. Do you understand?"

"Perfectly."

"Where is this ciphertext?"

"I don't know."

"Do you, Marina?"

"No."

"Victor, you and Thereon have given me a great deal of trouble." Cornelius' voice still sounded gentle. "I am displeased with both of you."

"Sorry," said Victor. "But there comes a time when I can't go along with you and neither can Thereon."

"I wonder which one of you corrupted the other?" mused Victor. "Thereon is the younger, but I sometimes think he has the stronger character."

If Cornelius was trying to draw Victor, he did not succeed.

"I am sure he has," said Victor affably. "But I have a little more experience than he has."

"Experience of what?"

"Life, work."

"And love?" Cornelius glanced at Marina. "You really should take better care of her."

This did make Victor angry. Marina could see the effort he was making to hold his tongue and keep on smiling.

"Well." Cornelius put out his cigarette in a handsome malachite ashtray rarely used in this room where smoking had become infrequent. "Quentin told me that Marina got the ciphertext from him rather cleverly." Cornelius smiled at Marina and she thought it was the coldest smile she had ever seen. "What did you do with it?"

"She gave it to me," said Victor. "And I lost it."

"My dear boy, I am not a complete fool. I shall not believe

anything you say about its being lost, mislaid or destroyed by anybody. And I shall certainly not believe you if you say that you gave it to Thereon. He has no need of the written process, as you know, but you do. So . . . where is it?"

"Cousin Cornelius, you still don't understand Thereon and me, do you? We are not going to let you have Vortex."

"Really?" Irony and contempt were nicely blended in one word.

"Really." Victor was on the point of losing his temper now.

"Why?"

"You know why. We told you days ago."

"You mean all that pacifist nonsense? Are you seriously suggesting that while every other nation is arming to the teeth, we should deny ourselves sophisticated armament?"

"No, I am suggesting—seriously—that we should not sell Vortex to possible future enemies."

"Oh, yes, I'd forgotten. You take the patriotic line. It's Thereon who takes the pacifist line. Of course you're both fools and there is no medicine for a fool." Cornelius sighed. "The only thing that really counts in life is power. That's what drives men who make fortunes. The pleasure they take in power, not pleasure itself."

"Is that why you want Vortex?" demanded Victor.

Cornelius seemed at a loss for a moment, as if he had never thought to examine his own motives before, but he rallied quickly. "I want Vortex because it is mine. My money made it possible."

"And the brains of five scientists who died when a plane crashed in Iran."

"I can buy all the brains I need or want," said Cornelius. "The one thing that is hard to get is money. It commands brains and everything else. Thereon has corrupted you with his peace talk. War is man's oldest social tradition, and we must all learn to live with it."

"There's nothing traditional about this new laser."

"Why do you and Thereon have such a prejudice against it? I think it's a godsend. Now, if it should become necessary, we can have a preemptive strike, like Pearl Harbor, without fallout. The war will be over in twenty-four hours."

"And what will be left?"

Cornelius retreated to a prepared position and mounted a firm defense there. "We don't even need the real power to make a first strike. All we need is to make other nations believe that our first-strike power is real. Then we'll have international stability."

"Stability? Through a balance of terror? Fear is the most unstable thing in the world. All you need then is one failure of nerve, and the fat is in the fire."

Victor walked over to the big window. He stood still for a moment, looking up at the prehistoric light from the stars, then wheeled to face Cornelius.

"You don't really care about your son at all, do you? Suppose I did hand over the one written record of Vortex that still exists? Would that change Thereon's situation for better or worse?"

Cornelius would hardly have lit another cigarette so soon after the first if he had not been feeling some strain.

He took a deep draft of smoke and glanced toward Marina. "Does she know all about Thereon?"

"No."

The magnified eyes behind the thick lenses focused on Marina speculatively. There was something chillingly impersonal about that gaze. Suddenly she realized what it was.

She did not exist for Cornelius as a person. She was only a thing, a counter in some intricate game he was playing. Whatever claims she had on the fellow humanity of other men or women through youthful comeliness, through intelligence or character or affection, did not exist for him. She was simply a tool to be used, a pawn to be sacrificed. She was as certain of this now as if he had shouted it at her, and she knew he would sacrifice his son or his wife as easily.

Even the criminal and the insane usually have some link with one or two other people, but Cornelius was totally alienated. Talking to him was like talking in a vacuum. There was nobody there. For human personality is response to society and he who cannot respond ceases to be a person. Cornelius was a spiritually invisible man, a ghost. His gentleness was not courtesy, but apathy.

Even now, while he was trying to win Marina to his point of view, his voice was detached rather than persuasive.

"Long before the atom bomb, J.B. S. Haldane wrote in his book *Daedalus* that the real empire-wrecker today is not the statesman or general, but the scientist, a 'poor, little scrubby, underpaid man' whom no one has ever heard of. A year ago five such men, working in one of my experimental stations, developed a laser that could be made to bend. The moment I heard about it I knew I had the supreme laser weapon.

"I started a new company, Luka, Incorporated, with offices and workshops near Boston, and I put your husband in charge. I spent large sums of money, and part of that money went to maintain a very tight security.

"I was not afraid of governments. I was afraid of other multinationals. Mazda agents have been after Vortex from the beginning. Quentin Yardley and his men managed to hold them off for a while, and then my luck turned. That jet crashed in Iran."

"Mazda?" said Victor.

"Of course. They tried to force the plane down so they could capture the scientists alive, but forcing a plane down can be tricky. All the scientists were killed, and all the papers they had with them were burned. Luckily we still had some copies of the basic manufacturing process in the Boston office of Luka. The problem then was how to protect that secret process from further sabotage or theft.

"I came to Boston to discuss the question with Quentin. I stayed overnight at the Ritz, and the two of us met in my rooms. Quentin kept vetoing every suggestion that I made. He kept saying: 'Mr. Skinner, it just isn't good enough.'

"I was standing at the window, looking at the Public Garden across the street, when he asked me: 'Are you going to see your son, Thereon, while you're here?'

"I answered: 'Yes, I'm dining with him in Cambridge this evening,' and then it hit me, what Quentin was driving at. You see it, too, don't you, Marina?"

She looked at Victor, who was frowning; at Cornelius, whose face was as bland as ever.

"I'm sorry to be so stupid, but I don't."

"It's not stupidity," said Victor. "You just don't have their kind of ruthless imagination."

Cornelius went on in that same detached voice which he never raised no matter what the provocation.

"Perhaps you have forgotten that Thereon is a prodigy? A living computer who can do mathematical problems in his head in a few seconds? Problems that it would take you or me hours to do with pencil and paper?"

163

"You and Cousin Anna did say something about that when I was in Connecticut."

"Prodigies like Thereon are able to perform these parlor tricks largely for one reason. They have total recall, whether they realize it or not. Thereon realizes it. He knows he can glance at pages of numbers or equations, quite meaningless to him, and still remember every detail a year later or ten years later without a single mistake. It's just as if he had an instant camera in his brain."

Marina was beginning to grasp the implications of this. Shock left her breathless.

"You mean that you and Quentin got Thereon to memorize the Vortex process so it didn't have to be written down in any form that could be stolen or destroyed?"

"They did worse than that," said Victor in a rock-hard voice. "They didn't tell him what he was memorizing. They let him think it was some trifling industrial gimmick that nobody cares about. He had no idea that people all over the world would harass, torture and kidnap him for a secret like this."

"Don't exaggerate, Victor," said Cornelius. "Today such people often use drugs or hypnosis."

"But they prefer torture because it doesn't distort memory. Did you warn Thereon that he would have to live in fear? Did you tell him that he would never be able to trust anyone again? No, you treated him like a dog. You tied a tin can to his tail and let him run, run, run to get rid of something he can never lose. It was not from you but from Mazda agents who tried to bribe and intimidate him that he finally learned the truth."

"That's one thing I don't understand," said Cornelius. "How did Mazda agents know that Thereon had memorized the process? You didn't know about it until after Marina had her accident. Only three people knew about it then, Quentin and I and Thereon himself."

"There's always a leak somewhere," said Victor. "How did Mazda find out about five scientists flying to Iran on the same plane?" He turned to Marina. "Now do you see why I put the Vortex process in cipher? Thereon told me the whole story when I was ordered to Iran because he thought I would be in danger there. I tried to think of some way of protecting him.

"He was in danger only as long as his memory was the sole repository of the Vortex process. Threats to him could be parried if I had a written memo of the process which Thereon could use to buy back his life and freedom. This memo had to be in the most indecipherable encicode I could devise, for if it were no longer a secret it would lose its value as a bargaining point."

"Exactly my point of view," said Cornelius. "We should be working together. We both want to protect Thereon's life, and we both want to keep the Vortex process a trade secret."

"But you also want to sell Vortex to the highest bidder in the open market," said Victor. "Thereon and I don't."

"Thereon and you can't even agree on a common policy," returned Cornelius. "He wants to destroy all records of Vortex. You want to hand Vortex over to your own government without bargaining. Both ideas are impractical. Money is not made that way. And now I really have wasted enough time here."

Cornelius rose. "Where is Thereon?"

"I don't know."

"You're lying."

"What are you going to do about it?"

Cornelius looked at Marina. "Will you tell me? I'm sure you know."

"I'm not going to say anything."

"In that case—" began Cornelius.

Victor interrupted. He was standing with legs apart, hands on hips, eyes bright and dangerous-looking. He looked down at Cornelius. "If Quentin Yardley and his thugs lay a hand on Marina or Thereon or me—"

He never finished, for that was the moment when the front door opened again and Anna walked into the room.

She was in black, her suit as dark as her hair, her face as white as her blouse.

She knows, thought Marina. She's always known. That's why she's always angry. As I thought before, it's her way of expressing fear.

She ignored the others. Her eyes were on Cornelius.

"I've been waiting long enough in that car. What have you been doing? Where is Thereon?"

"I haven't the slightest idea. They won't say."

"Can't you make them? He must be here. Ronnie?" Her voice was louder but its tone was less harsh. "Where are you, dear?"

She had left the door open. Now Quentin Yardley appeared in the doorway. Beside Victor he looked like a weak carbon copy.

"Shall I search the place, Mr. Skinner?"

Cornelius shook his head.

Anna turned to Victor. "Won't you help me find him?"

"Sorry, Cousin Anna. I have to say no in order to protect Ronnie himself."

"Can anyone protect him now he carries that Vortex thing in his brain like a malignant tumor? He must be here."

166

She hurried into the kitchen, but she was back in an instant making for the hall. They could hear bedroom doors open and close, her voice calling.

When she came back, her glance swept the living room again, lingered on the big windows for a moment, came to a full stop at the head of the stairs to the lower floor.

"I didn't know there was another floor."

Victor tried to stop her, gripping one of her wrists. "Please, Anna. For Ronnie's own sake—"

"Let me go!"

He had not anticipated the strength she could call upon to wrench her wrist free. She hurled herself down the stairs, Victor at her heels, Marina and Quentin following.

Anna reached the bedroom door first.

Marina closed her eyes. They should never have let Thereon hide down here where there was no door to the outside. She didn't want to see him cornered and humiliated now.

But when there were no sounds at all, she opened her eyes again. She looked at the bedroom and could hardly believe that it was empty. Even the bed was neatly made as if no one had slept there tonight.

"He's gone," sobbed Anna. "And—"

She was cut off by the sound of a car starting in the driveway.

As Marina had been one of the last to come down the stairs, she was one of the first to reach the top now with Victor close behind her.

Cornelius was still sitting in an armchair like a spectator at a play. Perhaps he lacked the energy for active pursuit.

Beyond the open front door, Cornelius' big, black car was backing down the narrow, curving driveway. Light from the house passed over the young face behind the wheel. Thereon.

"How . . . ?" began Marina.

"He got out of a window, of course. And he had to take his father's car because it was the last to arrive here. It was blocking both the others. Come on!"

Victor caught Marina's hand and pulled her into the car he had come in, Thereon's.

Marina thought: if it were not for our old, country habit of leaving ignition keys in cars parked in a friend's driveway, none of us could get away so quickly now.

Already the big, black car was backing out of the driveway into the road at a right angle. There was a clashing of gears as it roared forward and vanished around the next curve.

A wail came from Anna. "He forgot to turn on the headlights!"

Quentin Yardley lumbered across the driveway as Victor's engine started. "Wait. I'm coming."

Victor backed and turned his smaller car in the driveway itself and sped toward the road.

Marina looked back.

Quentin had run halfway down the drive and stopped there. Anna stood in the doorway, her knuckles against her teeth as if she were stifling another sob. There was no sign of Cornelius, yet Marina was sure that, if Thereon was recaptured, it would be because of some strategy Cornelius was thinking out now while the rest of them were spinning around a corner onto Route 117.

"Do you suppose Thereon heard everything we said?" asked Marina.

"He heard enough to make him run."

Far down the road they saw the red taillights of a big black car.

"Isn't that a Rolls?" said Marina. "If it is, we'll never catch him."

"We've got to catch him."

Victor stepped on the gas.

Chapter Fifteen

A winding road like 117 does not lend itself to hot pursuit. Every time the car ahead came to a tight curve, its tires squealed and their own tires echoed the squeal a moment later.

"We'll all be killed," said Marina.

"We can't lose him now," said Victor. "There's no knowing where he would go or what he would do if we did."

"Isn't he headed for Route Twenty and the rotary?"

"Probably, and there's no way we can tell whether he's going north or south until we see what he does at the rotary."

"There seems to be another car following us."

"What kind of car?"

"All I can see is the headlights."

"Better keep an eye on it."

There was one car between them and Thereon's as they swung onto Route 20.

"Why not toot your horn?" said Marina.

"What good would that do?"

"If Thereon looks back and recognizes his own car—"

"He'll probably go faster."

"He can't see I'm driving. Someone else might have grabbed this car."

"Cornelius?"

"No, Quentin. I doubt if Cornelius remembers how to drive now. He acquired a taste for being chauffeured during the war when he had a staff job and a sergeant used to drive him everywhere."

The rotary was a giant snail shell outlined in lights. Cars swung around its involutions peeling off at diverging tangents. They looked like outsized beetles scuttling for cover after someone had raised a stone where they were sheltering.

Sodium lamps leached color out of the scene. All the dark cars looked black and all the pale cars looked white. When the Rolls followed a curve below them which brought its profile into view, even its distinctive hood was hard to pick out in that synthetic half-light.

"That car behind is leaving us now. Going north, I think."

"So it wasn't following?"

"Apparently not. Can you see Thereon now?"

"I've got my eye on his license plate. Connecticut numbers are easy to read, blue on white."

Victor was holding his car in the middle lane so he could veer quickly whichever way Thereon chose, right or left.

A huge sign read TURNPIKE, SOUTH. At that speed it seemed to be rushing toward them while they stood still.

The black car cut to the left in front of them, squeezing dangerously between two other cars. Victor had to signal and blow his horn before he could follow the sudden turn.

"South? Why?"

"God knows."

Both cars had to slow for the ramp, built for twenty-five miles per hour, but Thereon with better acceleration slipped into the traffic stream before they could.

"Can we catch up to him at the tollbooth?"

"Maybe."

It was one of those unmanned booths where the driver pauses to snatch a card from a machine and goes on as quickly as he can. Thereon was through and on his way before Victor could bring their car to a halt.

"If you go through without grabbing a card, won't an alarm ring and bring the police?" asked Marina.

Victor grabbed his card and the little car jumped forward. "Do we want the police to stop Thereon now?"

"It's one way to slow him down and get him to talk to us. He's driving like a maniac now."

Victor took his eyes off the road long enough to spare her a sharp glance.

"So you've forgotten."

"Forgotten what?"

"Thereon still has the Vortex memo in his pocket, unless he's destroyed it in the last few minutes. We don't want police or anyone else to catch him with that on him."

"But it's in ciphertext."

"You broke the cipher. The police could find someone else to do so."

"Then what do you want to do?"

"From the beginning I've had two motives in all this. First, to keep Vortex out of circulation. Second, to see that Thereon does not suffer for what his father did to him."

"Do you think Cornelius suspects that Thereon has the ciphertext now as well as his memory of the process?"

"Quite possibly, but there's nothing Cornelius can do about it at the moment."

"I don't see him now."

"Thereon? His car's four cars ahead of us now. I'm holding back purposely. I want him to think we've given up the chase. If he sees we're still following him, he might be tempted to do something foolish."

"What do you mean?"

"Marina, haven't you realized what Thereon is most likely to do?"

"No, I haven't. What?"

"It would be awfully easy to crash that car."

"Oh . . . no . . ."

"Oh, yes. Think a moment. If the ciphertext is destroyed and Thereon's killed, that's the end of Vortex for several years, perhaps a decade. A delay like that might give the world the breathing spell it needs to come to its senses. Thereon is young. He still believes in such miracles. And then there must be the very human desire to get the better of a father who has used him cruelly and selfishly. I don't want to see Thereon thrown away."

"Of course you don't, and neither do I. Have you any idea why he's going south now?"

"I've been wondering about that. He may be heading for New York. It's the crossroads of the world. You can go anywhere from there, and there's no legal charge against him. There won't be anybody watching airports or piers for him."

"What about money and a passport?"

"He knows he can always get money from Anna or me. If I were he, I'd take a freighter for Costa Rica or Hong Kong. We're getting near Sturbridge, the exit for Hartford and New York. If he turns off now . . . Here we go!"

The Rolls had passed the tollbooth before they reached it. Victor accelerated. Both cars were swept into a network of back roads, unwinding through woods and farmland, villages and small towns where street lights were few and every house was dark at this hour before dawn.

Five minutes later they had lost him.

"I was afraid this would happen when we left the turnpike," said Victor. "Shall we keep on?"

"What else can we do? We just might find him."

Now the New England landscape unfolded before their eyes in seemingly endless repetition.

Tree-shaded streets; old white houses clustered around grassy commons with duck ponds; little churches with steeples so sharp it was hard to tell whether they were aspiring to God or defying him; the occasional factory town with its dreary, miniature slum and abandoned railway station; the supermarkets which had long ago replaced the old general stores; the Victorian mansions, with the largest and handsomest always occupied by a bank or an undertaker; schools with spanking new buildings and lavish playgrounds; the weekly newspaper in a basement office down a dingy side street . . .

How vulnerable they looked, these little towns locked in sleep under the stars, just before dawn, their houses dark, their streets empty.

Marina thought of laser missiles descending out of the night without warning on little towns and villages as vulnerable as these all over the world. She felt like crying aloud: Wake up! It's almost too late. . . . But who would listen?

"Asleep?" said Victor.

"No, I wish I was. We're not going to find Thereon, are we?"

"Doesn't look that way, but— What's that?"

As he spoke he pulled the car over to the edge of the road.

"What's what?"

"There's something over there."

They got out.

The road here seemed to run through the middle of a big farm. There were cornfields on one side, sugar maples on the other. A rough track, hardly more than two parallel ruts in the ground, led from the road in among trees. Under low branches a car was parked without lights.

"It's the Rolls," said Victor. "And it's empty."

They walked over to it and tried the doors. All four were unlocked. There was no key in the ignition, no evidence of a struggle, no sign of Thereon at all.

"Let's look around."

They explored the woods. They even crossed the road and ventured a little way into the cornfields, but they found nothing.

"Should we notify the police?" asked Marina.

"Ronnie may not thank us if we do. He probably ditched this conspicuous car on purpose and is now hitchhiking to New York. We might as well go home. We can breakfast on the way."

"And the car?"

"We'll call Cornelius later in the morning and tell him where it is. I have a feeling he wants to keep the police out of this, too."

"Why?"

"Publicity is probably the one thing in the world he is afraid of."

"I wonder how he and Anna got home?"

"Your car was still there. Quent probably borrowed it for them."

The only place they found open for breakfast was an all-night stop for truck drivers.

Outside in the parking lot fierce, anticrime floodlights turned night into day. Inside, the huge place was like a cave. A few low-watt bulbs made little impression on dark brown walls and a high ceiling lost in shadow.

At the counter a fly circulating happily inside the plastic cover of a pie dish discouraged appetite. They ordered only orange juice and coffee.

On the stool next to Marina sat the only other woman in the place. She was short and sturdy with hair cropped like a man's. She wore a man's jeans and shirt and sweater, and she was polishing off a plate of ham and eggs with a man's gusto.

She met Marina's glance with a smile. "Yes, I'm a truck driver. Independent driver-owner. Not many women in this racket, but I like it. I'd die if I had to work in an office with all the gossip and backbiting and all the money you have to spend on clothes."

"Don't you ever worry about being alone on the road at night?"

"Not me. I believe in camouflage." She reached down under her stool and pulled out a man's felt hat. She put it on her head, pulled down the brim and winked at Marina. "See? When you're driving at night the only thing folks see through the windshield is an outline. With this hat and my short hair I show them the outline of a man. Of course, I'm probably just as capable of taking care of myself as most men, but this trick saves me bother."

"It's clever," said Marina. "I'm going to try it myself sometime."

"You'll have to cut your hair, if you do."

•   •   •

When they reached Lincoln the stars were fading one by one as if someone were turning off lights. When the last star had gone, the sky was no longer black sapphire but gray, almost white. The color was paling so gradually that change was imperceptible at any one moment, yet by the time they reached their own house the sky had become the clean, light blue of an Italian primitive's heaven.

As if this were a signal, birds began to call good morning to each other in cheerful, conversational tones. Against the chirruping, one faultless singer lifted his voice high in a piercingly sweet hymn to the newborn day.

"Is that a lark?" said Marina.

"Don't ask me. I'm city-bred, too."

Victor unlocked the front door.

As they walked into the hall, a face appeared above them at the head of the stairs.

"Thereon!"

"Hello, Ronnie. We thought you were halfway to Hong Kong by this time. What happened?"

He didn't answer either of them. He moved forward one clumsy step and held onto the balustrade to steady himself. He was not usually clumsy. His face was pulled down now like a tragic mask. His eyes burned as if he had a fever. His lips trembled.

Marina started up the stairs, but Victor put out a hand to stop her.

"What's the matter, Ronnie?" said Victor. "Why don't you come downstairs?"

"I . . . can't."

"Why not?"

Thereon looked back over his shoulder to the shadows at the head of the stairs.

"Come on, Ronnie." Victor allowed a hint of impatience to leak into his voice. "We've had a rough night and I'd like an explanation. How did you get in here without a key? If you don't come down, I'm coming up."

Another voice spoke out of the shadows.

"Stay where you are."

She stood beside Thereon now, at the head of the stairs, immaculate in jacket and slacks of Chinese silk brocade in brilliant jade green. Her skull cap of golden hair had never looked more polished and shining.

Marina found her voice. "Why, Lettice . . ."

"Be quiet."

It was then Marina saw that Lettice was carrying something in her right hand, a professional killer's machine pistol.

Even in that moment of shock, Marina noticed one small detail. Lettice held the gun as if she were accustomed to its weight and knew exactly how to accommodate the balance.

Chapter Sixteen

Someone was knocking on the front door.

"Let them in, Marina."

There was no friendship in Lettice's voice now. This was an order, curt and impersonal.

Marina moved slowly toward the door.

"Don't anyone make a sudden move. This thing is on a hair trigger. So am I."

Marina made every movement deliberate as she turned the door knob and pulled the door toward her.

Cornelius was standing on the step outside, Anna and Quentin a little behind him.

One look at Marina's face told Cornelius that something was wrong. She saw his eyes change and his gaze go beyond her to Victor at the foot of the stairs, to Thereon halfway down, and finally up to Lettice herself at the head of the stairs, still holding the ugly weapon in her shapely, well-cared-for hand.

Cornelius' little frown suggested irritation rather than fear. To a man whose only contact with violence had always been through layers of polite intermediaries, it must have been irritating to be thrust so suddenly into anything as raw as this. Not so much shocking as distasteful.

"You're Lettice King, aren't you?" he said softly. "You must have got to your own home just as Thereon was leaving. You followed him?"

"And gave him a lift when he got rid of your car."

"It was clever to bring him back here when you thought the house would be empty, but it's not clever to brandish firearms." He spoke to Anna without turning his head. "Wait outside."

"No." It was the first trace of emotion Lettice had shown. "You must come in here now. All of you."

Cornelius turned to Anna. "That seems to be an order, my dear. I'm afraid we are in no position to refuse."

Then, incredibly, he offered her his arm.

The archaic gesture was the one thing he could have done with grace, Marina decided. He could hardly invite Anna to precede him in advancing upon a machine pistol, and if he had stepped in front of her suddenly Lettice might have opened fire on both of them.

Quentin followed them hesitantly into the house, the guard dog frustrated by a crisis outside the pattern of his conditioning. He had not been programmed for a situation where friends suddenly became foes, and charming young women who met his employer on terms of equality brandished guns. Just as we delight in recognizing any familiar pattern, we suffer when the familiar takes on an unrecognizable shape.

Alone Quentin might have risked rushing Lettice. He could do nothing with five other people in her line of fire, including Cornelius.

It was Cornelius who broke the silence.

"Mazda, I suppose?"

"Of course." Lettice smiled.

"We did wonder who was their principal agent here. I never thought of you."

"I did," said Victor. "But I had no proof."

Marina remembered then that Victor had never liked Lettice. She remembered thinking about that in the clinic. It was Lettice who had recommended Lincoln to them as a place to live and found a house for them there as near her own as possible. Was it Lettice who had suggested taking Marina to the Sanders Clinic after the accident?

"Oh?" Lettice did not turn her head toward Victor or even her eyes, but she was listening to him.

"Fashion modeling made an ingenious cover," said Victor. "I suppose it was as genuine as Sanders' psychiatric cover and, like his, was established long before someone from Mazda involved you in espionage. Did you recruit Sanders? Or did he recruit you?"

"Does it matter?"

"Not really. You had to kill Sanders because he knew you had tried to kill Marina, and he was going to give you away to the police so he could bargain with them to save his own skin. After all, he was only an accessory after the fact."

"Lettice . . . you tried to kill me?" The enormity of the idea was beyond Marina's grasp. Would she ever trust anyone again?

"Didn't you guess?" There was scalding contempt in Lettice's voice now. "You are an ingenue. My assignment was to get Vortex from Victor. Mazda learned he was being sent to run Luka in Boston months before he himself knew. Mazda tried bribery and intimidation. When neither worked, they called me in to make a more personal approach.

"I was well on my way to success with Victor in New York when the unpredictable happened. He met you by accident and contracted that lunatic marriage with you. Of course I kept on trying, but the marriage was too new for me to make much impression on him. Sexual attraction is as illogical and inconvenient as any other stupid fixation

"I soon saw I couldn't get anywhere with Victor as long as you were alive. So you had to go. It was the only way I could carry out my assignment. It would have worked, too. What man is more susceptible to the attentions of any sympathetic woman than a newly made widower? And I was a little more than just 'any woman' to Victor."

"You fell in love with him, didn't you?" said Marina.

"Me? Love? Don't be ridiculous."

"I still can't believe it," said Marina. "I never suspected you. I trusted you. And I did see a man driving that other car when it hit mine. . . ."

"Or did I? The light was dim. All I really saw was the silhouette of a man's head. Your hair is as short as a man's. It could have been you wearing a man's hat in order to mislead anyone who saw you.

"When I didn't die, I suppose it was you who suggested to Victor that I be sent to the Sanders Clinic where your friend, Eric, could drive me to the edge of sanity? Did Mazda deposit the fifty thousand in Victor's account where I found it after he disappeared? Was Mazda still trying to bribe him after every other approach had failed?"

"So what?" said Lettice. "I didn't come here tonight to discuss all this. I came to get Vortex. Eric Sanders told me before I killed him that there is one written copy left, a ciphertext. I want it. Where is it?"

"You can't have it," said Thereon.

182

"Oh, really?" Lettice flashed a brilliant, bitter smile at him. "You told me a little while ago that your name is Thereon Skinner. I've heard whispers about your total recall lately. They say your father is using you as a repository for his most valuable trade secrets. No matter who has the written ciphertext now, you must have the ciphertext itself in that innocent, adolescent head of yours. If you do not give me what I want in the next sixty seconds, I shall kill you."

The hand that held the gun was steady. The eyes were merciless.

"Oh, no . . ." cried Anna.

Thereon returned Lettice's smile without bitterness.

"You don't know what you are doing," he said. "But you are liberating me."

He threw himself at her. They fell and rolled together down the stairs. At the foot, she freed her hand and pulled the trigger. She was still pumping bullets into him as he died.

It was Victor who numbed her finger by striking her wrist with the edge of his hand so that Quentin could wrench the gun out of her grasp. The first burst of fire had destroyed Thereon's unique brain and erased the Vortex process from its neurons forever.

Cornelius sat down as if his knees had suddenly given way. His face was gray-white.

"May I borrow your cigarette lighter?" said Victor.

"I didn't know you'd gone back to smoking." But he handed over the lighter.

"I haven't." Victor took a folded paper from a pocket in Thereon's shirt, laid it in an ashtray and set fire to it.

As it curled into ash, Cornelius said: "What's that?"

"The last of Project Vortex," returned Victor. "And the least I can do for Thereon."

Cornelius then made his only comment on his son's death.

"We shall have to start Vortex all over again from scratch." An inspiration came to him. "You could be of invaluable help in that, Victor."

"You've forgotten something. I resigned some time ago from all association with Luka, Incorporated, and Skinner Industries.

Marina crossed the room to put her arms around Anna.

"Don't say anything," whispered Anna.

Marina held her until the police doctor came with his sedatives.

The sun was high in a bright blue heaven before Victor and Marina were alone.

"What now?" he said. "Shall we go abroad for a year?"

"Oh, yes . . . if we can afford it."

"Let's go whether we can afford it or not."

Postscript by Helen McCloy

In 1944, when I was writing another book about ciphers called *Panic*, I read something, somewhere, about a cryptological double bluff, a two-step cipher in which the first of two enciphered texts was as coherent as a cleartext. Theoretically no cryptanalyst would break the cipher because he would not realize the second step was there.

When I was writing *The Impostor* in 1976, I wanted to use this little known, two-step cipher, but I was unable to trace it. In despair, I decided to risk improvising my own version.

It was the most difficult thing I ever did. Perhaps it is no wonder that an associate editor of *Cryptologia*, Mr. Cipher Deavours, discovered three flaws in my presentation of the cipher. He was kind enough to write me a letter suggesting how they could be avoided without altering my story-line. It is too late now to amend the text in either the American or the English edition, but not too late to add this explanatory postscript to the English edition.

The criticism falls into three parts. First question: how could Marina produce a two-step decipherment of the cipher using the same slide alphabet each time? How could this be done without changing the key each time? Answer: the key is changed each time though this is not stated explicitly in the story. I arrived at the two random, running keys I used by inverting the usual enciphering process. Knowing the cleartext and the ciphertext, I was able to pair a clear letter and a cipher letter on the Saint Cyr ruler so they then generated their own key letter.

Second question: how could Victor possibly memorize two long, incoherent keys? Answer: as I see it, he would keep a written record of the keys which he could destroy, if necessary, relying on Thereon's total recall to recover the keys afterward. Mr. Deavours himself has made a most ingenious suggestion for avoiding some of these difficulties. In the first step, when the cleartext is the laser formula, use the French song as the running key. In the second step, when the cleartext is the French song, use the first step ciphertext as the running key. I wish I had thought of that myself.

Third question: given a running key cipher, how could Marina, or anyone else, break it by using mathematical analysis alone on one short message? Here I can only cry *peccavi*. I suspected that a two-step cipher with two running keys, might be practically unbreakable on the basis of one short message, but I was not quite sure of it, so I decided to take a chance that Marina might be able to break this cipher with a combination of mathematics and intuition or, as Mr. Deavours suggests, ESP. This is not as far-fetched as it sounds. Many doctors believe that exceptionally gifted diagnosticians are guided as much by a sixth sense as by reason. Cryptanalysis, like medicine, is an art as well as a science.

One question remains: has this form of two-step cipher ever been used before? On page 131, I played safe by having Victor say it had been used "only twice as far as I know". That was based on my shadowy recollection of something I read in 1944 which I have been unable to trace since. If any reader knows anything about the previous use of such a cipher, I should be most grateful if he, or she, would let me know. Otherwise the whole thing will probably remain a puzzle for the rest of my life.